OTHERWISE KNOWN AS POSSUM

OTHERWISE KNOWN AS POSSUM

Maria D. Laso

Scholastic Inc.

Copyright © 2017 by Maria D. Laso

This book was originally published in hardcover by Scholastic Press in 2017.

ISBN 978-0-545-93196-0

10 9 8 7 6 5 4 3 2   18 19 20 21 22

Printed in the U.S.A. 40
This edition first printing 2018

Book design by Carol Ly

Chapter 1

CROWS ALL FLAPPY

Around here, when folks die, people cook.

Fried chicken, corn chowder, sweet potato pie.

Trouble is, then they put on their Sunday clothes and take that food to the home of the dead person.

'Course, the dead person can't say boo, much less eat.

The family of the dead person can't talk nor eat neither. How could they, on account of all the sorrow storming inside that drowns out every noise? Plus the big rock stuck in their throats, the one that keeps down the howling, but that's hard to get food or words past.

So what happens is, the people in their Sunday clothes stand around visiting with other people in their Sunday clothes, all of them eating that food they brought.

Dredged catfish, potato soup, ambrosia.

They talk about things like Mister President Hoover and the sad state of the country and will that Mister Roosevelt set things right. Everyone talks about the election coming and the drought going and where there might be work. Everyone talks about things that won't matter to the dead person. Things that shouldn't matter to the dead person's family.

Eventually, the people in their Sunday clothes get tired of standing in their Sunday shoes, so they leave. Every one of them hopes at least this many people will do the same when he passes.

With the last of the Sunday-clothes people gone, the house hushes past silence. The dead person is still dead. And the people left behind have to find the way and the will to crush the quiet before it crushes them.

That's why I was sitting under Momma's tree, shooting windfall pecans at the crows with my flip. I knew Momma, most of all, would expect me to smarten back to usual in no unhurried way, even if the crack in my heart would never heal.

As a rule, I do not shoot at birds, but crows are trouble, a nuisance that will eat crops and gardens. Crows don't even sing for supper.

I put another pecan into the band, pulled tight, and aimed, squinting right between the Y and one tick to the left.

Traveler whuffled.

I could see the crows' beaks move, but they sounded like old biddies minding someone else's business.

Trav snorted, lifted his head, and gave a grinding sound from his deepest parts. He stood rigid, peered over my shoulder, and then pulled on my coveralls.

The Town Ladies were back: It was them Traveler'd heard. They'd swooped onto the porch, all black wings and beady eyes like giant crows, beaks fixing to stick into our business.

I considered taking a shot. After all, a crow is a crow, and I have dead-keen aim, on account of I am naturally gifted for such things. Plus, I have the finest flip a person can have, made by my daddy, who is a wonder with all kinds of wood. He's good at everything he does; he just doesn't do everything.

Instead, I pushed my glumpy pigtails out of my eyes and followed Traveler to see what had been in the Town Ladies' claws. Our noses told us covered dish. Smelled like creamed corn 'n' onions.

Momma and Baby died in June, and it seemed like every week in the two months since, anyone who came calling brought black-eyed peas or *pileau* or crawdad fritters. Only, the more people who came by, the lonelier I felt.

Used to be I was never lonely. Even when I wasn't with my best dog friend or my best person friend, my days were filled with the music of creek splashing and idea hatching and life living. But it got quiet when we lost Momma—she was the music Daddy and I danced to.

Now birds sang, hens still cackled their fool

heads off each day, as if nobody ever laid an egg before. Yet always I seemed to be waiting for laughter, for crying or calling. Everything felt cottony. At times, I feared breaking apart from aloneness, but other times, I needed to get alone quick for fear of bursting.

In all that haze, there were only three things I could be certain of:

1) Trav is the best dog ever.

2) I can count on my best human friend, Tully, till Kingdom Come comes.

3) Daddy needs me to keep us keeping on. Momma would be counting on me from Heaven to keep any more change from ripping apart what's left of our lives.

I peeked in the front window. The curtains were drawn, so I couldn't see in, but I could picture those pink-powdered Crows perched around Momma's front room with the creek-mud walls and hand-sewn pillows and the company chair.

I could hear them well enough too, thank you kindly, chattering things like, "Surely the girl..." or "For LizBetty's sake..." and "...neighbors in your time of need."

They were all-fired fixed on telling Daddy what to do. And not just what to do, but what to do with *me*! "Mister Porter, that child needs proper schooling."

Talking like I wasn't there. Never mind that I wasn't.

"Why, we have this lovely young teach—"

Whose voice was that? I strained to hear.

"I'd say she's young. I wonder why she didn't marry but left kith an' kin to come here. One of those Roosevelt Reds, I imagine."

"Ladies, please," came a new voice, stronger and louder, Miss Nagy's. "We agreed to present a united front for Mister Porter. The fact is, a young girl left without a mother, particularly in these, um, rustic circumstances, why, she's going to need someone to see to a proper education."

Proper education? I took their squawking to mean schooling and that steamed me, it really did. I am past eleven and a half, working on twelve, and never been to school on account of I know everything my momma taught me, and she knew more than anybody.

In the pause that followed, I pictured the ladies rearranging skirts and strategies. I figured the biddies were, as usual, ruffling the air with their words.

Daddy had yet to say a word, but of course he had no more mind to send me to school than he'd ever had. And why would he? Momma was clear on the subject. She said knowing comes from every kind of person and place, and she believed in learning over schooling. To me, who's been learning up and down the holler my whole life, school'd be as wasteful as a bath on Wednesday.

Besides, Daddy and I had an understanding: No more change. I wanted things like when they'd been perfect. I wanted to hear Daddy's hammer out back so I could picture Momma taking him cool spring water, her about to walk back into the kitchen, where the smell and sound of her was more than a soft pinching at my heart.

But he was all but gone, that Daddy who'd pick up Momma and spin her for no reason beyond air is for breathing. A shadow of a stranger who looked like him had been put in his place. He'd been spending more time than ever in his shop, and though woodworking is his language, I wasn't sure what he was trying to say. And I sure wasn't going to figure it out by spending all day in some *schoolhouse*.

But life lately seemed frailer than morning webs, and everything seemed sideways. Maybe this new-thinking Daddy would be flapped by those old Crows into turning against Momma and toward Town Ladies and teachers and all manner of Trouble with a capital T.

I couldn't sit around waiting to see. I had to get

the old biddies to leave before they turned Daddy's head.

It was high time they got a taste of their own medicine—tea as sweet as those salted old biddies.

I sprinted down to the creek to pull two cool jars of pale amber tea from the creek cooler. I ran one across each cheek and then carried them around back to the kitchen door.

My eyes lit on Momma's favorite apron still hanging from a wooden peg. From the parlor Daddy's voice floated in—the same voice he used to reason with GrandNam when she would not be reasoned with. "Noralee took schoolin' serious," I heard him say. "And she had her own ideas about it, that is for sure."

I pulled down jars and glasses that hadn't been used since the funeral and set one on each flower of Momma's painted Chinese tray like they were blooms of glass. Then I poured cool tea into each like I was a Robin Hood bee returning nectar to each blossom.

Daddy continued, "Point is, ladies, meanin' no disrespect—by my mind, the decision's made— and not like to be altered by you. And it has nothing to do with her learnin' so far. Possum does sums in her head faster'n me—you all too, probably. She read to me and Noralee by the time she was four."

Truth. We only had a Bible, catalogs, and tired magazines from Newcomb's, the general store on the county-road side of town, but I read it all. That was a big part of Momma's idea about schooling versus learning. Momma explained more than once, "In a school, you learn everything between four walls. I want you to learn the world."

Often I'd read to Momma and Daddy by kerosene lamp while they snuggled up on the porch, her back fitting into his chest, his arms around her waist. 'Course we made up lots of stories too. Through stories and pictures, we saw worlds on worlds.

With the contents of the second jar poured, each container on the tray held about three fingers' worth of two-day tea, which is made by adding boiling water to used leaves and setting the jars in the sun. Two-day tea is just right for pulling the steam out of you after a long walk or a fast run.

From the second shelf by the stove I took down the pink glass sugar bowl, its handles stuck out like Connie Harris's ears. I used both hands, like Momma showed me, and took it by the bowl. I held it up to the window and marveled, like I always did, at the way the light goes through the bowl's feet and makes tiny rainbows on the walls.

I added to the tray a stack of napkins hemmed by GrandNam and ironed into fierce fourths by Momma. Finally, I took down the tin shaker that sat next to the sugar bowl, listening for the rustle of the rice grains.

Daddy said, "I'm not sure now's the right—" But he cut off when I backed into the room with the tray of refreshment.

The ladies looked real surprised, Daddy even more.

I managed not to look at him while I set the heavy tray on Momma's good library table and offered around tea, each glass delivered with a napkin to catch its damp ring of sweat.

"Why, thank you, dear," said one Town Lady.

"Aren't you thoughtful?" chimed another.

I studied Momma's rug, hoping to seem lady-like, but, church-truth, it was so I wouldn't bust a gut. Long as Mister President Hoover had us Americans Hooverizing for the good of the country, wouldn't I be downright unpatriotic to waste good sugar on the likes of those old Crows?

The oldest Town Lady, Miss Nagy, raised her glass first. She was sitting on the davenport—well, really, it's a daybed with pillows—so she did not have the angle to notice that I had neglected to serve Daddy.

I snuck a look around one pigtail at him. His eyebrows were shot to the top of his head, asking me something.

Miss Nagy swallowed, and her puckered face

got puckerier. Her eyes squinted, then opened, opened big, crossed. Tea blew out her mouth and nose. The Crows flapped in consternation and dismay, gagging, coughing, or sputtering.

Daddy, the only one looking my way, pressed his lips thin, but I thought I saw laughing eyes. "Possum!" he said in his warning voice.

Miss Nagy looked at me over her spectacles, a fierce stare. "That tea is full of salt, young lady. Do you have something to say?" Her eyes looked like they alone could brand my hide, yet I knew she believed that she believed in forgiveness.

I stared right at her. "I want to apologize for putting salt in the sweet tea." It was my humble voice.

The murmuring resumed, and Miss Nagy nodded once, almost like she believed me.

"It's just—just—" I pushed my bottom lip out a bit.

Daddy slumped like the air was punched from his lungs. "Possum? What's wrong, sweetie?"

I looked away quick. "It's just, someone musta moved the"—sob—"I know Momma kept sugar in the pink"—sob—"but salt? I don't"—sob—"I—"

Not a single lie.

I was backing through the room as I talked, looking with my humble face into the craggy faces of each biddy as I went. Every one looked at me like I was the baby lamb instead of the coyote. Except for Miz Pickerel, who was making faces into her serviette. I figured she must still be trying to rid the salt from her mouth, as she was not likely on purpose making such faces at Miss Nagy's back.

"Well . . ." Miss Nagy began.

Next I covered my face with my hands till I felt the weather in the room change.

"Thank you for understanding!" I said as I neared the doorway that would be my escape. "Now, I reckon I ought to see to those delicious-smelling dishes you all so thoughtfully brought. Won't you excuse me, please?"

From the kitchen, I heard a bit more squawking and murmuring. "It's just this kind of behavior . . ." That sounded like Miss Nagy, long past hopping mad and on toward leaping. I pictured her standing, curved like a question mark so her spectacles teetered on the wart with one hair in it.

"Now, Miss Nagy, the poor creature has just—"

Then Daddy's voice came through like Preacher's on Sunday: "That child *is* a creature, ladies, a creature of God, perfect in His sight. Nor do I appreciate the suggestion that the upbringing Noralee and I have provided has failed her."

I felt my chest puff for making Daddy proud, yet I was spitting mad at them for suggesting Momma didn't teach me right.

"Oh, now, we didn't—" That, I knew, was Miz Pickerel's quiet, Karo-syrup voice. She was a young widow, her face less crackly than the others'.

As their discussion went on, I realized my trick hadn't done what needed doing. Just like crows, they'd flapped and squawked and ended up landing right where they'd been. I needed to shoo 'em away before they mentioned any more of that school nonsense.

Then something familiar caught my eyes in a new way. Daddy shaved in the kitchen, where the window had the best morning light. His strop and mirror hung on a post by the sink, cup and brush on the ledge. They gave me an idea.

I passed the brush across my lips and cheeks. I love the feel of the soft bristles and the soap smell. A couple drops of water in the cup, and I worked up a right good lather. Then I opened the screen door to Trav, who had been whimpering outside. For the piece of bacon I slipped him, I was paid in kissy slobbers. Then I set to work, foaming up his jowls till he looked like Santa Paws.

As I washed up, Traveler nosed around. I let him sniff another piece of bacon before I put it in my pocket and raced him into the hall. While keeping Trav back with one foot, I dragged my little stool in front of the swinging door. I knew Trav would get it open once he set his mind to it.

Thanks to the bacon, his mind seemed set to it.

I put my pocket against the crack and let Traveler sniff once more, for extra double-sure good measure. Then I went back in to see to the Crows.

"Ladies," I said, walking slowly to the far end of the room. I cleared my throat.

Daddy glared me a warning, which I conveniently did not see. He had his ways to punish without using a belt or peach-tree switch. Sometimes, when I had not been the best, he would refuse me a candy treat or a nighttime story, and did *that* hurt. He'd never given me a lickin', but I figured that could change directly.

Lucky for us, that look was as far as Daddy was able to get before a clatter pulled him to his feet. "What in tarna—"

Twitchy Miz Pickerel flapped like a jitter jack.

Then Traveler was jumping at me for bacon, his foamy beard flying every which way, and chaos erupted.

Aww, wouldn't you just figure Tully had to be away to miss the sight of it? I sorely wished he'd been witness, because he was not likely to believe the telling of it.

The Crow Ladies ran squawking out of our lives, which serves them right for what they tried to pull, disrespecting Momma and all the learning she'd given me.

I knew Momma would be proud that I'd bested the old Crows while also giving Daddy the chance to say that Momma's way was the right way. We had no need to change anything, especially what wasn't broke.

Chapter 2

BUNDLE of BROWN

I opened my eyes when the floorboards outside my door creaked. Daddy stuck his head in, and I saw right away he was shaved, hair slicked back wet.

"Up, girl. Wash your face. Come on."

Before I could make a peep, he was gone, Trav at his heels like Daddy's boots might be made of bacon. But when I smelled breakfast, I dressed just as quick.

In the kitchen, Daddy was serving my favorite, biscuits with bacon fat.

Trav, his "rabies" all cleared up, stared at the pan like it held GrandNam's punkin' pie, his favorite.

"Go on, Traveler," Daddy shooed. "You know better'n that."

Trav sulked away.

I ran my hands in the pump water and wiped my face before sitting in my own blue chair. I'd got so I could do it without hardly looking at Momma's lonely yellow one. Still, I swallowed hard at the sense in the air of something. Again.

Instead of meeting Daddy's eye, I watched Trav's tail dip between his legs as he curled into his cold-weather spot by the stove.

"What's going on, Daddy?" I asked, wishing I didn't feel like I had to ask. I was tired of surprises I didn't know anything about.

It's what I'd spent most of the night thinking about. If Daddy and I were going to keep our little family together, including a place for Momma, we needed to keep everything just like it was.

Every change, even tiny ones like being woken early on a Sunday, could be trouble. I did not want one more freckle to fall off my knee for fifty years. At least.

"We're goin' to church."

Church? Well! That's just the kind of unexpected that you don't mind when it finally gets here. "Why come, Daddy?" I'm partial to the singing and rainbow windows though not the wearing of shoes.

Daddy put two whole biscuits into his mouth and held up his wait-a-minute finger.

I used the time to try to recall where my funeral shoes were. Under the table, the toes of one foot tested the size of the other. Maybe my feet had grown. Maybe the wretched shoes wouldn't fit. Or we wouldn't be able to find them. Or, best yet, Daddy wouldn't remember I had shoes at all.

Luckily, I'd had a bath just last night, singing to Momma from the tin tub till the sky darkened and skeeters outnumbered lightning bugs, but that was coincidence. I no longer got to church regular. I used to go with GrandNam. She and I went near everywhere together, and her favorite was church.

'Course, now that Momma and Baby are in Heaven too, I reckon GrandNam can catch up with Momma all she likes plus get to know Baby, maybe take him to meet David in that green pasture with the still water.

Daddy wiped his damp brow with one of the kerchiefs I washed for him weekly and finally answered my why come. "Let's say we're going to thank God for autumn and pray for cooler weather. Plus, you can thank Him that I haven't found wherever you had Traveler put those shoes of yours."

I'm of no mind about people's feet one way or another, but GrandNam made sure I had shoes in church. Though I reckon God knew what my toes looked like, and so did Preacher, as he saw 'em plenty when I helped Daddy build the choir risers.

On that sweltery September Sunday, Daddy and me and my bare feet walked up the silent, hot, country road with no more words needed between us. I felt that we would present a united front to the Town Ladies in front of God and all, and they would see how things are. That he and I were doin' just fine and didn't need any more of their fixing.

Yet I knew those biddies likely would keep flapping back, poking at Daddy. Crows are constant. He might eventually want to give in, just from weariness. So I'd take my cause to the pulpit, so to speak, and be sure every man, woman, and child I encountered in the holler knew I was already good for learning and in no need of schooling.

Every critter path eventually leads to water, but for people, their ruts and roads seem to lead to salvation. Soon we were calling halloos to the neighbors' neighbors, all headed toward their weekly reward.

For plenty of folks, church, market days, and funerals is about the only times we see each other, but I knew not to look for Tully. He goes to his cousin's every summer or whenever his daddy finds himself in trouble too deep, but Tully can't ever get far enough to quit his place in me. When I had chicken spots, he did too, and we played cards for three days and itched each other's scratches. Both of us ended up with a scar shaped like a carp on our left shoulders. Makes us battle brethren. I wished he was on duty with me now. It was like I was half myself, which should have felt half the sorrow, but that I seemed to have twofold.

Not that Tully likely would've been along on any Sunday. His pa is like the prodigal son. Someday Mister Spencer will walk into church, and Preacher will call for the fatted calf. Till then, fall through spring, Tully works most Sundays at the distillery, which I might too if I wasn't in God's sight.

The closer we got to church, the lousier the path got with the usual saints and sinners, what Momma called the blessed in their best, and the bless-ed rest.

Taking in the social swirl, I hummed to be sure I'd be in fine voice, but a whistle slipped out when I spotted a cloud of dust rolling up the road, trailing a bundle of brown on two wheels.

When the dust cleared, what got my attention next was the short wavy bob of brown hair under a brown felt hat. Most grown-up ladies I've ever seen wear their hair finger-curled or in a pug, like is natural. But I saw in a magazine that city girls and movie stars are getting boy haircuts, and I wanted one, thinking it'd be less bothersome than knots and tangles. What I truly wished for was a scalp-mowing like the Justice boys get every spring, summer, and fall. 'Course, if wishes were matches, you could set the world afire.

Mostly I can't be bothered one way or t'other about hair any more than about shoes and feet. Momma used to fix mine; Daddy tried but once. "Hangman's noose, Possum," he swore. Took him forever to fix those "braids" and an entire summer twilight to unfix.

When I finally tore my stare from the new lady's hair, I fixed on her brown skirt and shirtwaist; even her eyes blinked brown at the world. My eyes are brown too, like Daddy's, melted chocolate. Hers, though, look like cedar, not the bark but the inside, at once warm and splintery.

Brown Lady parked her bicycle and put right her hat, smiling at the Crows flocked and fanning in the slim river of shade near the church steps. 'Course, Momma is the prettiest lady I've ever seen, including in picture shows, because those ladies don't have the wild roses of Momma's cheeks or the smell of the lavender sachets she sewed and planted around our house.

Still, this lady looked . . . well, not painted like those movie stars but not dried up and dusty like the ladies around here neither. I felt I knew what Preacher meant by scales falling from my eyes. She seemed young and fresh-looking despite the dust along the hem of her skirt.

As Brown Lady stepped forward, the Crows folded in close, almost as if they thought the steps were a nest that needed protecting.

I wanted to get closer. Any stranger is news, and any news is bound to blow something interesting with it. Truth, we don't get many strangers at our Church of Good Endeavor and Intention. And this one didn't look like any I'd seen. Surely a lady who looked so soft like that couldn't be *so* dangerous?

Miss Nagy stepped forward the way I figured a missionary might face a pygmy. With righteousness in the heart, nothing in your face can give away what you might be feeling to see something so fearsome and strange.

Though the biddy's face was stern as cracked earth, at her words the Brown Lady lit up like the Fourth of July. I imagined Miss Nagy didn't know what to make of the stranger's damp forehead and perfect white teeth, much less the sight of her bicycle or her ankles.

The old biddy pointed in the direction of the road, by where Daddy stood. Probably telling the young biddy to leave, right away making me want to invite her in. Isn't that what Jesus would want? I at least wanted to get close enough so I could give Tully a full report. He'd be sorry to miss the sight of this passerby, even if she weren't a customer for his pappy's still.

At that precise moment thinking about her, as I sidled close enough to use the ears God gave me, the Brown Lady turned my way. She was sure-enough pretty and didn't look like a menace—yet when her smile fell to Daddy and he half nodded back, it made me feel hot and funny.

As Daddy caught up to me, he seemed about to speak. Instead of letting him, I grabbed him by one sleeve and pulled him toward the church steps.

Inside, the smells of soap and clean sweat and lilac water rose to greet us. Though Mrs. Preacher played the upright as folks drifted in, the flutter and sigh of ladies' fans were louder.

I took Daddy's hand and let him lead me to our regular pew near the David window—my favorite. Seeing the little shepherd boy and feeling Daddy's hand in mine, I felt for a moment like I belonged in a place—a feeling I didn't even know about till I lost it when Momma died.

I did not see whether the Brown Lady sat or even came in, because Daddy made me stop twisting around to look. "Who do you think she is, Daddy? What do you think she wants?"

I figured that if she dared to come inside and she *was* a she-devil, the piano music would thunder, giving us all fair warning. To bide my time, I studied David's stained glass lamb and loosed up my tongue for hymn singing.

GrandNam said singing is a kind of prayer. Personally, I'd think during church is when God is busiest and doesn't need to hear any more requests, so mostly we talk under Momma's pecan tree. Still, when the organ wheezed itself awake for "Joyfully Reunited," I made sure everybody I know in Heaven could hear. What proper lyrics don't land on my tongue in time I fill in with my own:

When autumn's chill puts trees to sleep,
When winds are cold and snow lies deep,

Our father's love will keep us warm,
Our spirit strong and safe from ha-a-a-rm.

I wasn't the only one with a mouthful, because when the music ended, someone kept singing. It was only a few extra notes, but it was no intentional solo by one of Preacher's kids. And mine wasn't the only head turning to find the source.

Those of us who did look saw Brown Lady holding that last clear note, eyes closed and chin raised. Only when she appeared good and sure that that final prayer was all the way out of her mouth did the stranger open her eyes and close her lips. That she seemed to take no more notice of the looks or whispers than I might made me smile.

Who is she?

By the time Preacher Andrews gave one of his less fiery sermons about how the Good Samaritan today would vote for Mister Roosevelt, and Mrs. Andrews read a six-page letter from a Texas couple we sponsored on their mission of mercy to Darkest Africa, and Susie and Diane Andrews led a three-hymn prayer session intended to persuade God to break the blessed heat wave by mentioning "river" or "water" or "streams" or "washing" about 837 times, I had to crisscross out of church with my knees together and hightail it to a place I could relieve myself.

Next I followed a row of ants carrying leaves ten thousand times bigger than their heads. I decided to help them out by putting a whole pileful right outside their hill; it's what Christian neighbors do. Hopefully, they did not have to labor so long and hard on their Sabbath once they discovered the miracle of the leaves. Maybe they would make a parable about it.

By the time I'd wandered back toward the church, it appeared most everyone had gone on to the social hall for Philco time. With batteries expensive and hard to come by, anybody with a radio has a day to turn theirs on for whoever cares to listen, and naturally on Sunday it's God's turn, by way of Preacher. Most folks bring picnics and stay right through Chase and Sanborn Hour.

I made my way toward Daddy, who was talking with Big Mac and his dad, Little Mac, knowing they'd be talking something good: fishing or hunting, crops or job prospects. Turned out to be election talk. The Macs are about the only folks left in these parts who don't think "Hoover" is a cuss word.

While I waited, I used my toes to make a row of rocks, two deep, across the dirt path, nosing them into order with my big toe while mostly looking up at the trees and whistling snippets of hymns.

I know God sees every sparrow, but I had not

anticipated He would notice my little wall of Jericho until Brown Lady's front bicycle tire tumbled it. I barely had a chance to laugh before she wobbled right into Daddy, who saved her.

Tully's pa, who knows a lot about women cuz he doesn't have a wife, says some women act weak and helpless so a fella will feel the need to protect them. I think that's disgusting. Nobody was less weak or helpless than Momma, and I ought to know, because I turned out just like her. Everybody ought to take care of themselves, is what I think, and not live off someone else, like ticks on deer.

She climbed off the bicycle after Daddy grabbed hold of the handlebars, and he said something to her and looked my way. She smiled but did not look at me. That alone seemed curious enough for me to investigate.

I watched the Macs tip their hats at the lady and then scurry past me, headed in the other direction as quick as I've ever seen them move, like the Brown Lady had a medicine they didn't want to swallow. This made me even more curious.

"Rather warm, isn't?" She fanned herself with the gloves she carried.

"No more'n we might expect"—Daddy twirled his hat in his hands—"this time of year."

She used the gloves to shield her eyes and looked up at the cloudless sky. "I hope rain will bring some relief. I'm sure the crops and such could benefit as well."

Couldn't this stranger tell Daddy was no farmer?

"Rain brings its share o' troubles."

She switched the gloves from one hand to the other. "Yes, of course, it does. Too much of a good thing can become a bad thing, can't it? That would be true of most things."

"I wouldn't know about most things, miss. Just wood. Don't guess you can have too much wood." With each word, Daddy seemed to be backing away from the Brown Lady even though his feet weren't moving.

I felt my eyes rolling in my head. I've seen one season chase the last while grown men talk weather, weather, and more weather. This seemed to be more of the same, to my great disappointment.

Then I glanced toward the Crows, and the way their heads bobbed, sharp and stern, made me think. I've learned a lot more about rabbit hunting by minding the fox than by watchin' the rabbit. And right then that nosy Miss Nagy and the Crows were eyein' that Lone Ranger lady, hungry as foxes.

I sidled thataway. "City-slick, I'd say. Hope she don't intend to fill our children's heads with poems and communism."

Communism? Communing with who? I wondered. But poems, I like those. They're like Bible verses but with more music to the words. I spotted a ladybug stumble and tumble while trying to climb a little mound of loose dirt.

"Far as I know, she has not so much as lifted a ruler, not even to that willful Whitman boy."

To who? To who?

"Heard she's real smart. Got her own technique for keepin' them in line."

"Ruler never did no harm."

The ladybug fell to the bottom of its hill again.

Won't hurt to get closer. I nudged the ladybug back up her hill. If I accidentally heard something more, well, so much the better.

I heard those old Crows call Brown Lady a lot of things, some of which I didn't understand. One I did know was "New Yorker."

Was she a Yankee? If so, she was my first. That would explain, I supposed, her looks and ways and the Crows' suspicions. I studied her closer. For sure it was not normal or regular for a grown-up lady to ride a bike to church. And there was the simple fact that she was here before us at all.

"I'm sure I don't like the way she's standing so—" Had she ever ridden in a fast car? Did she know any loose women? Had she ever seen an elephant?

"Maybe they do things different up north. Though you have to wonder—"

Her Sunday best didn't look faded or worn nor did it resemble any of the simple dresses someone like Momma or GrandNam might have worn to church.

"'Course, that Roosevelt woman is to blame. Mannish, if you ask me, and—"

I snuck another look at her face. Maybe her nose looked a bit citified, once I thought about it. I looked toward the ladybug again just in time to see her fly off.

"I heard the schools up north teach that socialist Mister Kipling! To children!"

Danged if I knew what half of it meant. I felt dizzy with wondering about the strangeness I could see and even more about the strangeness I could not see because it looked like regular people. Then again, you don't always know you've found a good fishing hole till you spend the day fishing it.

"Poor Noralee barely cold, but that's a man. Like a starling and a shiny spoon—"

Hearing Momma's name seemed to break the spell this stranger had cast on me, and I forgot the bicycles and elephants as I tried to decide whether they were saying Momma was the starling. Or was it Daddy? Or this Yankee?

"—and his poor daughter still running wild in the woods—"

Suddenly, Brown Lady clapped, and her smile could have melted bacon fat.

Just as suddenly, the Crow Ladies seemed to notice me and each other. With knowing looks, they dispersed to whatever craggy old swamps they'd no doubt flown out of.

I was surprised to see Daddy also smiling, something beautiful I had not seen near enough of since Momma died. I did not at that moment wonder what this Yankee person had said. I only knew it wasn't right for him to be giving away a smile that should've been for Momma.

Chapter 3

BUGGY LADIES
and LADYBUGS

Daddy motioned to me, and with some considerable effort, I at last made it the ten long paces to where they stood.

The lady in brown held out to me a slim hand gloved in soft tan leather and said, "How do you do, LizBetty? I'm your new teacher."

I tried not to let her voice, which was soft and brown like that shirtwaist, into my ears. At that moment, I realized she was nothing but a gussied-up crow.

"My name is *Possum*."

My voice, to my own ears, didn't sound so much harsh as brave. When the Brown Lady held out her hand to me, it flinched, which made me feel even braver, brave enough to bury my own hands deep into my own pockets.

"Possum!" Daddy chided.

My toes took on a fascinating quality I had not before been aware of.

The Brown Lady at last withdrew her hand, yet it didn't feel like I'd gained the advantage. Perhaps it was better to ignore her altogether. Ignore her words, which surely announced Daddy's betrayal.

"Daddy, we should be getting on home. Trav'll be worried."

He looked stopped up, but he turned to *her*, not me. "Like I said to you before, miss, her ma was the only one called her LizBetty. Mostly we call her Possum."

It was on account of GrandNam that everyone called me Possum. When she died, I got our bed to myself. Except for summer of course, when we sleep outside. But our bed was too small without her in it, and every morning, I'd wake curled on the floor. Daddy took to calling me Possum. Momma said "Possum" was no kind of name. She always said LizBetty, which is my given name. She picked it herself.

The stranger made her lips tiny. "Is LizBetty a diminutive?"

Daddy shrugged.

"My name is Miss Cordelia Jane Arthington," she said. "Is LizBetty short for a longer name, Elizabeth, perhaps?" She sounded like she very much hoped my name was short for Elizabeth Perhaps. Which it is not.

Daddy shook his head. I speculated maybe

he was struck mute after this enormous act of betrayal so close to the church.

Yet she pronounced slowly, like she was thick or thought we were, "Well, Possum is certainly no kind of name for a young lady."

Momma's very words! Yet how they stung coming from this stranger in brown.

"If you don't mind"—she leaned down again to look into my face—"I will call you LizBetty."

I hacked up as big a chunk of ammunition as I could muster considering how dry and tight my throat was.

Daddy squeezed my hand hard, more a warning than reassurance.

I tried to pull away my hand, but Daddy held on tight. My head rang like when you're too close to a shotgun going off.

I allowed a jumble of fast and quiet words—none mine—to continue another minute, and the next I knew, the bicycle rode away. From behind, she looked like a skinny brown circus bear.

At last, Daddy let go, but his look tugged me off toward home. His mouth was set straight as a pin as he looked for words on the horizon. He'd start to speak and then sputter. It was like he weren't sure of the thoughts jangling around in his very own head. I'd never seen him in such a state.

What had that Yankee devil done to my daddy?

Finally, I could stand no more. "Daddy, you ain't swayed by those Crow-pies and that teacher lady into thinkin' I need to go to that school?"

He near stumbled even though he was staring hard at his own feet.

"I reckon I need to do some thinking," he said.

I lagged behind, dragging my feet and kicking up dust just like bulls when they're fixing to charge, but Daddy took no notice, his jaw clamped tight.

Soon as we got home, Daddy had but one word for me. "Beans." And then he shut himself up in his shop.

I stomped up the steps and dropped next to the bushel basket of green beans, pulling an empty basket of like size between my knees. Hornet-mad as I was, I snapped the ends off those pods in the blink of an eye.

Years past, Momma and I could make such a job last a full summer's evening. It was the only good thing about shucky beans. But now I'd be the one with the long needle, threading the pods onto twine to hang in the root cellar to dry. Come winter, I'd be the one soaking them overnight, and I'd be the one cooking them. And there'd be no Momma to tease me into eating one more dry, chewy mouthful. And no Momma to save me from the bad learning of school. Was there no end to the misery before me?

I clomped into the kitchen, letting the screen

slam behind me. Except instead of making me feel better, the silence that followed cut. It should instead have been Momma reminding, "LizBetty Porter, you are not a tornado," making me go outside and come in "like a lady."

But if there was no Momma, what difference did it make?

Making as much noise as I could because I could, I added flour and water to a bit of leftover squirrel stew and set it on the warming stove. I chopped up a whole onion, glad to let my eyes burn and water. I stirred the spit-colored pearly bits into the stew and then smacked the ladle on the edge of the pan. Daddy doesn't care for onion. But. That. Was. Too. Bad.

Trav whimpered and crawled under the table.

I was still stirring and smacking when I heard Daddy washing up at the pump. While I'd snapped and stirred and steamed, I'd also been preparing. I stiffened my spine and my chin and willed them to stay strong for me when I needed them most. I practiced what I needed to say: "Daddy, I want nothing more to change."

Daddy'd caught me unawares before, but I felt as ready as I could be. If Lee and Jackson could take Chancellorsville with one Gray for every two Blues, I reckoned I could face Daddy armed as I was with hot dinner and cool reason.

The lumpy mess of greenish-brown stew smelled

even worse than it looked, but when Daddy came through the door, he didn't seem to notice. Before I could even open my mouth, he put his damp hands on my waist and lifted me easy as those ants lifted a leaf at church that morning. *Lordy, was that today?*

Daddy set me—a bit too firmly I thought—on my own blue kitchen chair. "Possum," he began, and his face took the shout from me. "I love you as much as any man can love a daughter. More. That's how I know those old biddies had one thing right."

I knew what was coming as sure as GrandNam knew it would rain without seeing sky. But it was not beyond me to use whatever skills I had at my disposal, considering everything at stake. I put out my bottom lip far as it could go and let Daddy see it tremble.

I tried the words I'd rehearsed. "Daddy, I want nothin' more to change."

"Me neither, baby girl."

He turned away. Hallelujah! I felt like the worm let go on his way to the hook, wriggling with relief, but he turned back a moment later with a cup of water. "Drink this."

"But—"

"But buttons," said Daddy quietly.

I drank.

We each considered the other.

"Life is change," Daddy continued. "Nothing stays

still a moment longer than it takes to realize the moment's gone."

No question. Life was changing. I felt like a freight train was heading for me, and I was helpless to get off the train track.

"I know, Daddy." Nobody knew better'n me the way summer became fall, and then winter, then spring no matter how much you might wish for even a bit of change.

He scraped a chair across the floor and sat knees to knees with me. "Honey, I know you don't want to go to school, but, well, you're going, and that's the end of it."

The choke in my throat seemed to meet an ache in my chest and blocked everything from going in or out. I couldn't think. I couldn't breathe. Then the air rushed in, and the words rushed out.

"Daddy, I *can't* go to school, even if I wanted to," I reasoned. "For one, who'll make supper?"

"I reckon I can cook well enough," he said, taking from me the ladle that was still in my hand and setting it on the table.

"For two, who'll scratch your back when you're done working?"

That was Momma's job, and she had taught me, like she taught me everything.

He had no words for that, for clearly he knew it was true.

"For third, what will happen to the perfectly

good learning from Momma that's safe between my ears like the black eye on a pea?"

Nobody was going to unteach me only to fill my head with foolishness.

"For four," I said, lowering my voice, "I heard stories about that teacher. I heard some kids went to see her and were never seen again! I heard when she looks at little kids, she licks her lips and cackles! I heard—"

"I believe," said Daddy with a small smile, "that your hearin' is too sharp for your own good. I'm sure that teacher's no witch, and if she was, I doubt she'd be the type to eat children." He stood and reached for the ladle on the table. "Those witches are generally green."

Who knew Daddy knew so much about witches? I couldn't wait to tell Tully.

"'Sides," Daddy went on, "you so bony, I don't guess you got anything to worry 'bout. You'd be slim pickings, indeed."

Daddy chuckled, the little lines by his eyes rippling like water. It was as much of my own Daddy as I thought I might ever see again, but in a tail flick, he got serious again, looking into my eyes. He didn't seem to notice he still held the ladle.

"Listen here, Possum. A young lady, which you're gettin' to be daily, needs to be 'round women, to learn womanly things."

I smelled a bluff and jumped in.

"Well, for five, then. Who's to say this Miss Arthington *could* teach me these mysterious things girls *supposedly* ought to know? *If*, like you say, I'm getting to be a young woman day by day?"

Daddy sighed.

"Which anyways I am not prepared to say is factual, 'cause how come Momma never mentioned it? It feels more like a trick from those old Crows."

He set the ladle back on the table and took my earthy hands in his work-dark, whistle-clean ones.

"You need to be around a lady, honey pie. You don't want me to marry any of them old Crows, do you?"

This terrible thought that had never entered the Eden of my mind now hung about like the serpent in the apple tree. Yet somehow still Daddy talked and the world hadn't spun off its axle.

"So I reckon you ought to go with that new schoolteacher and learn what you can."

A heavy breath went out of me, and all I could think was to pull away my hands. I turned so as to not look at him watching me and didn't mention Traveler pulling the ladle off the table.

More good reasons to stay home came into my head, but my jaw stuck.

And at last I knew it was too late when he said, "It's what Noralee would want. Learning's learning, and seeing as she ain't here to see to it . . . I don't see as there's any other choice."

Then he stood and walked away. He was moving so slow, like an old lady buying yard goods.

Part of me wanted to run after him. The rest wanted to throw the stew at his head.

Traveler, ladle in his mouth, scratched the floor in front of the screen, so I followed him out to the pecan trees.

Bird-songing and bug-buzzing must have been about, yet I couldn't hear but a howling wind. Judging by the still of things, it was in my head only, same as I heard when Daddy told me Momma had gone to Heaven. That time I stopped hearing anything else—or talking—for two whole days.

I wondered, as I'm sure Daddy did, why it had to be Momma. She never hurt anybody. She fed any trainmen that came by—she didn't like for us to call them "hobos." She let them eat on our back steps after splitting wood or fetching water. Momma said men keep pride in their throats, and if they don't work for it, their food won't go down right.

If I accidentally hit a songbird with my flip, which I'd never do on purpose on account of how Momma loved their music, she'd fix his wing, or help me bury him.

I paced around Momma's tree, fussing and fuming. Finally, I sat like clabbered milk gone from angry to sad, thinking on Teacher and those old Crows circling around me and Daddy.

If anyone cared to ask, I could show we were

doing just fine, thank you, and had no need of nosy noses and meddling meddlers.

Trav came back, mud-pawed but without the ladle, and laid his head in my lap. I ran my hand down along his black-and-tan back, back up, ruffling the fur, then down one more time to smooth it. This was my special hello. Then I scratched that place between his ears, and he snorted "thank you."

"Momma, please ask God to change Daddy's mind."

I figured Momma was in good with God on account of her regular going to watch the night come. Still, I didn't want to seem pushy in case God was listening, so I added:

"If He can't do that, well, maybe knocking down the schoolhouse would work. Just till we can talk Daddy out of this foolishness."

Another thought came to me. If I needed to learn so-called women things, maybe instead God could turn me into a boy? I wouldn't have to go to school but could work with Daddy all day.

But—as usual when there's more questions in your head than teeth, as I had regular—there were no solid answers. But I just knew somehow, I had to make Daddy see: School would just wash Momma's teaching from my mind and heart like a washboard worries at a stain. And no matter what, that was the one thing I had to stop from happening.

At the ripe age of eleven-goin'-on-crazy—all questions and no answers. I couldn't see no way out of going to school, but I was already fixin' to figure out how not to stay there. Sure as shirttails, I'd be back home before Teacher or those flappy Crows could do anything else to pull me and Daddy apart.

Chapter 4

RIDE to the MOON

I went back to doing the things that needed doing, like shooing crows out of Momma's pecan tree and, when he'd let me in, helping Daddy in his wood-shop out back, among my other chores and daily travels. Felt like I had a good hold on things, so long as I didn't let my mind wander too much to what was or what could have been.

Laid out flat on my back, my head on Trav's side rising and falling with his breath, I watched fat white clouds move as slow as I felt. I recalled when Momma taught me about the circus parade in the sky, how the clouds formed dancing animals and flying acrobats just for her.

"Oh, Trav. When Momma was alive, I was a cloud, floating like nothing weighed me down. Now I feel so full of wishes I could sink in a rain puddle."

Trav yawned in agreement. Then he stood, knocking me to one side. He looked into the woods, meaning something was coming, but since his tail wagged, I knew it wasn't a bear or an Indian or a swamp monster.

He looked from me to the woods and back until I said, "Okay, boy, go on." Trav ran into the brush and barked once. A moment later, he jumped back out, and at his side was June May Justice, carrying a big old parcel.

"Hey, gal," I said. "Trav heard you comin' a mile away."

"I wasn't even trying for quiet." She dropped the package, and Trav stood, front paws on her shoulders. She grabbed his ears and whispered into one.

Anyone else, I'd be mad at them telling my dog secrets, but June May and animals is a different thing. She talks to them like they're her favorite people, and what dog, donkey, or duckling wouldn't appreciate that?

Besides, me and her are near family. She has never lied to me, stood me up, or let me down on purpose, and I'd stare down a grizzly for her, not that I'd need to since no grizzly would be rude to June May.

June May floated over, smelling like mowed hay and sweat, and plopped down next to me. Everything about June May seems to drift on invisible breezes. She's light as air, like a summer breeze, and as welcome. Seems there's always room for June May. She has wrinkly yellow-white hair that doesn't so much grow out of her head as float. Add in her eyebrows and lashes—the same shade of pale as Trav's—and she looks more than anything like a dandelion going to seed.

June May tilted her head at me and then set still except for her jaw. As usual, she was chawing on the braided strop she wears around her neck. I didn't have to see it to know it ended in a fine little moleskin pouch she'd made to hold the Lincoln-head penny what her daddy give her 'fore he left.

My daddy and June May's been friends since they were boys. Her ma, Miz Landy Justice, was Momma's best friend, excepting for me and Daddy of course. The Justices have six boys that lived, starting with Jump, maybe the only one among 'em with the sense God gave a muskrat. Plus, June May has a coon's compass for a brain.

She wiggled her skinny butt into the dirt and grinned at me.

"Where you headed?"

"Miss Eulah's." She rubbed her sweaty bangs first on one bony knee, then the other. "Wanna come?"

"Guess you might not make it if I don't."

June May was nine, near two years younger than me and stick-scrawny.

June May fiddled with the string on the package that flattened the grass between us. Miz Justice takes in what sewing and washing she can on account of Mister Justice being away looking for work, like so many other daddies and husbands "all across the blessed whole Hooverized United States of America, God help us and bring on Mister Roosevelt," as Preacher often said.

GrandNam said Miz Justice spins like a spider, fourteen stitches to an inch, so tiny and perfect they look made by nature. June May collects and delivers the bundles. Sometimes I help.

Jumping to my feet, I picked up one side of the parcel and, over my shoulder, whistled to Trav. When I turned, he was already in front of me. Darn smart dog.

A squirrel darted across the path. Trav didn't fuss at it but instead looked at June May as if to say, "See what a good dog I am? I would never hurt a poor, defenseless squirrel." Something about that girl brings out the best in all creatures.

We had the heavy load between us, holding the parcel by the string. It was cutting into my hand, but if June May wasn't complainin', I wasn't about to.

Instead, she was smiling, had been since we started off. A little secret smile to herself, because that's where June May lives most times, inside herself.

Trav bounded ahead, clearing our way of ferocious beasts but always doubling back to make sure we knew how hard he was working. He never goes more than a whistle's worth away.

"What'choo thinkin' 'bout, June May?"

Some folks, not me, think she's backward as her

name. Though I have with my own eyes seen her play for an hour or more with a paddle 'n' wheel, and that's just a tin circle nailed to a stick. If she lost the wheel, she'd probably be just as pleased to play stick horse and ride to the moon. At times, she disappears for hours, and if you ask where she's been, she gets that moony look and says not a word. Not even I know what she's up to half the time.

"What," I tried again, "are you thinkin' and grinnin' over there like a milked cow?"

June May turned like she was waking from a dream. "School."

I snorted on that sore subject. "What about it?"

"I'm glad you're comin' for the learnin' too."

Things were surely not right in the world if June May had gone to that wrong side of thinking.

"What you talkin' about? You know, sure as peaches in summer, Momma didn't want my learnin' boxed into that schoolhouse."

June May can be a bit simple, but I never worried too much about her on account of she can learn all the truly important stuff a body ought to know from all those many brothers of hers, including Jump, who is fourteen and about the best rabbit trapper I ever seen. But maybe I was wrong.

"I'm fixin' to learn to read."

The boys weren't ones for reading, that was true, though I'd learned plenty else from watching Jump and I'd tried to teach June May her letters, but her eyes don't see the same things mine do.

"For real this time." She opened her mouth like to say something else but closed it again.

"Well, that's fine, June May. When you do, you can read me 'n' Trav to sleep like Momma used to."

I twinged to think on that, but by then our foolishness had got us to Miss Eulah's place. I set the parcel on the step and rubbed my red hand. It felt good to have a different kind of pain.

June May ran up the porch. "Hey, Dusty, how's that ear, better?"

Miss Eulah's milk cow lives on the porch, in the shade, though Miss Eulah's usually in the sun. Right then she called out to us from the kitchen plot, "Miss Eulah be there d'rectly, girls."

'Course, Miss Eulah is about a hundred and her "directly" never is, so I drooped onto a step like a worn-out willow. As she shuffled toward us, I compared her sagging, tobacco-colored skin to my sun-browned arms. Miss Eulah rarely goes inside, because this way, she says, "When da Lord He fit to take me, He won't have't go lookin'."

Trav got himself a bellyful of cool water from the trough below the pump, while June May scratched between Dusty's eyes and whispered into what I figured was the bad ear. June May can't stand to see any animal or person hurting. It's plain inconvenient at times.

Trav curled up under the steps as Miss Eulah come up finally and heaved herself onto the lowest step, barely missing Trav's water-speckled snout. "June May, you hear from your daddy?"

"No, ma'am, not lately." June May fussed with Dusty. "Penny postcard a while back."

Miss Eulah nodded. "Tell your momma I had the Vision, and I seen he fine, got hisself good work over to Grant County."

"Yes, ma'am, I'll be sure 'n' tell her." June May beamed like she'd seen her daddy herself. In fact, he'd been away since around the time we lost Momma. "Milk in the crick house?"

Miss Eulah nodded, and June May ran off to get her bucket, which I pictured keeping cool in the shade of the little shelter Daddy built for Miss Eulah after she fixed my baby colic. Miss Eulah is a healer and, since she was a girl, has had a touch of the Sight. GrandNam told me so. The closer to blind Miss Eulah gets, the better her Sight.

June May came back with two tin pails, one half-full of eggs. "I best get these home. Come to supper?"

I'd been taking plenty of meals at the Justices since Momma died. I tried to cook for Daddy or him for me, but often as not he'd send me off with June May with flour for biscuits or some such, saying he'd fend for himself, though I don't rightly know how. No matter how hard I tried to take care of him, he just seemed to keep shrinkin', sometimes looking tight and hard as cured leather. Stood to reason that me going to school would just make Daddy shrivel into such a hard prune that no amount of pokin' would get through to the pit-stone heart of him.

June May set down both pails and squatted, rearranging the eggs like she had a plan. "Boys'll likely be there," she told the creamy shells.

"Well..." I wanted to ask Jump about his double-figure-eight follow-through knot.

Miss Eulah dumped a load of carrots atop the eggs. Don't rightly know how she does it without breaking a one, but she never has yet, and she grows enough to share with half the holler. Like our garden, which GrandNam kept fed with bits of sand, chicken litter, pine bark, and sawdust till the soil exploded in thanks, Miss Eulah's earth was more loamy than the clay-rich earth brought in by the river flooding its banks. Either of those ladies could and did grow just about anything from prize tomatoes to fresh asparagus and grapes plus roses and japonicas and even hostas that couldn't feed a bat at noon.

Last fall, Momma and I stacked a year's worth of carrots in sand under Miss Eulah's house. I think carrots taste best in winter, when you know they've finished working and are in bed asleep till you need them. These carrots, I realized, might remember Momma like I do. I'd come myself this year and stack every last one of them. No way Miss Eulah needed more change and hardship neither.

Taking a tiny cloth poke from one of her apron pockets, Miss Eulah turned her cloudy eyes toward June May. "Give this to yo' momma, hear?" She fumbled the little bundle of herbs into June May's hands.

"But Miz Justice ain't sick, Miss Eulah," I butted in.

"They's for the baby, child." I felt sick when Miss Eulah clasped my shoulder. "For the baby to come."

Part of my head knew Miz Justice was in the family way. Still, Miss Eulah's hand felt like a branch in a nightmare where I'm lost in the woods. I knew she was thinking of Momma and Baby. Not even Miss Eulah could save them.

Suddenly, I didn't want supper anyhow.

"As for you, child." Miss Eulah put her long thumbs on my cheeks and cupped her hands over my ears. "Don't be trustin' everything you eyes and ears try tell, hear?"

"Ma'am?" Her skin felt like dry paper on my sweaty face. Her breath was hot as Dusty's, only not as sweet.

"You look and listen heah." She poked my chest. "Don't be mixin' up learnin' and knowin'. Ain't that right, June May?"

"Yes'm, Miss Eulah." June May grinned at me, then at Dusty, then at Miss Eulah.

Miss Eulah kept hold of my head. "Now take me for a sample. I ached for proper schoolin' when I was the size of yous, but the hopes we hold ain't always the ones get handed to us."

"Why didn't nobody hand you schoolin', Miss Eulah?" Wide-eyed, June May pulled at the curl of hair that worried her nose.

"Some think only a certain collection of folk can be let into proper school on account of that's where all the knowin' of foreign lands is shared."

Miss Eulah gazed no place in particular, but it felt like she was seeing everything past and future all at once, and for a firefly-flick, she looked different, angry.

"Like el'phants, Miss Eulah?" asked June May. She's been stuck on elephants since I read to her in a magazine about Tarzan the Ape Man. We don't have anything around here like Hollywood or like the jungle.

Fast as a blink, Miss Eulah's angry look was replaced with her normal peaceable calm, and she nodded. "It's powerful, that kind of knowin', like Miss Eulah's knowin' is powerful, but sometime folks don't like to share it."

I tried to stop what was in my head from making my stomach flutter. Does it snow in the jungle? Do elephants like snow? All of a sudden I wanted to know useless things like what kind of footprints an elephant makes.

"I know every important thing." Didn't I?

But elephants. *What do elephants eat for supper?* I shook my head to free it of its foolishness.

The way June May and Miss Eulah was staring at me, owl-eyed, it wouldn't surprise me if their heads turned clear around on their necks. Those two were like to make me skeeter-crazy.

And then Miss Eulah said, "Possum Porter, you best git after that dog'a yours."

He'd been right at my feet. I peered down into the shade cast by the wooden steps my own daddy replaced two years back. No Trav. I turned in time to see a tail disappear into a stand of trees and blueberry bushes.

"See you soon, Possum," June May sang as I took off running.

"Trav!" I gave him our whistle, expected to see him bound back, but nothing rustled in the hot stillness.

"TRAV!" As I tumbled out of the bushes, I thought I caught a flash of his honey-velvet fur and spun around toward a brambly hedge. Moving this fast, he was showing more life than I'd seen— or felt myself—in weeks.

I heard a single bark a ways off and spotted a Trav-sized break in the grasses. Coming at it from the far side, I saw he'd hooked up with a critter path headed toward the hollow.

What's got into him?

I guess Traveler is about the best dog a person ever called friend, besides being the only dog I've ever had. When I had a fever, he licked my head till it cooled. Soft ears share the color and feel of giant pussy willows. And those eyes. Oh, those eyes. I know looking into them that he knows all my secrets, even the ones I haven't thought up yet.

"Fweeh-fweh," I whistled. "FWEEH-fweh."

Trav and me were raised together as pups, so he knows my mind, and I know his—usually. But he'd just taken off toward the hollow like he thought I was right in front of him, and that pure made no sense. Trav was *right there* after the funeral when I promised Tully I wouldn't go to our spot till he came home. We *spit-shook* on it.

But Trav wasn't coming to my whistle; all I heard was the sharp *whee-hyah* of a nuthatch making a party-line call.

That's when I lit out like a firecracker, *knowin'*.

I stumbled out of the brambles spitting dust and leaves and near about tripped on the roots of the giant oak that held our tire swing in its big branchy arms.

And there was Tully Spencer big as Christmas, riding our rope swing in lazy hawk circles.

"Aw, shoeshine," I swore. "Bullets and shoeshine." I needed time to know what I was feeling.

All summer I'd counted everything but chiggers

till Tully came home. Yet seeing that excuse for a straw hat low on his forehead, I felt tore in two.

On the one side, it felt like my shadow had walked into the sun and found itself.

On the other, what if he'd had all summer to get soft and start feelin' sorry for me?

The two ideas turned over and under in my belly like the seats on a double Ferris wheel while Tully just half-grinned down at Trav and me, him all calm as bees at midnight.

Hot and tuckered as I was, I could have shot straight up into the tree branches above Tully— and in good time too. But without knowing why exactly, I felt cantankerous, so instead I moseyed a mite around the tree trunk, giving my belly a better chance than it had had on the Flying Circles of Death.

By the time I rounded back to the swing side of the oak, Trav had settled into a good scratching from his favorite itching root. He opened his eyes to me all innocent, tail thudding on damp earth, before wriggling onto his back. "Traitor," I said, and right then I meant it. What kind of nonsense had my own dog turnin' his tail on me? I looked at Tully with suspicion—was he next to quit being his self?

Tully raised his chin at me, then went back to chewing sweet grass.

I couldn't think of a thing to say, so I didn't. Instead I inspected the cane poles that Tully had set up in soft earth downstream of our tree.

Some kind of time later, he said, "Hey."

Relief hit me the way a swimming hole meets a belly flop. 'Course I can count on Tully; he'll never let me down. I belched like a toad. "Hey back."

Tully stared at his feet awhile and then shot me a look. "Reckon you grow'd about a inch."

I guessed Daddy'd been too preoccupied to notice. Who knew what else I'd missed without my other eyes? A person needs someone to tell you such things.

I threw myself onto the creek bank, feeling tired of so many feelings piled on top of each other like ants in a hill.

Tully dropped from the rope and rolled down the bank, ending up on his back halfway between me and Trav. Dragonflies whirred the reeds like barnstormers till the buzz droned louder than my breath in my ears. I reached for the sack near my feet, figuring his Aunt Gree'd packed enough johnnycake for three Tullys.

Tully turned his head and spit out the grass stem, getting maybe two, two-and-a-half, feet on it before turning to look back at me. That's when I noticed that staring back from the rolled top of the sack was the angry-pansy coal-black face of the sorriest excuse for a kitten I'd ever seen. I tensed up and squinted at him, ready to run if he showed any signs of sap dripping.

"Found 'er under the bus stop. Some kids was pokin' sticks at 'er, but she's scrappy, brave. Figured she'd make a good mouser for Pa." He shrugged, but his eyes fixed on me. "Thought maybe I'd name 'er Possum."

My insides flopped like a landed bass; I couldn't look for fear of seeing those eyes people been giving me all summer. Pity-full. *Not you too, Tully.*

Tully popped a fresh stem into his toothy old mouth. "She got your fish breath."

A feeling started in me like a bubble at the bottom of a pop bottle and bust out my mouth. I laughed so loud and hard, like I hadn't done in forever, that our supper most likely swam itself downstream and into the next county. But it felt good to laugh, like the way it feels good to have a day of sun in the middle of rainy season, just when you think it's about time to build an ark.

Trav stood and barked once, wagging his tail to see me laughing, and Tully gave me that smile that told me everything I needed to know.

"Hear you been told to join us poor dumb folk in school."

Tully chucked the kitten under its pink-tip chin, and it was asleep in seconds, its tiny paws opening and closing in rhythm with its soundless breathing.

"So how you plannin' to get out of it . . . 'cause I know sure as anything you are."

Not surprising that we didn't catch a thing after all the hoo-ha'ing, but me and Tully had caught up and settled in easy as brown Betty crumble, and I was about halfway home before I remembered to stop smiling. My brain was still itching to come up with a plan . . . somethin' to make everything right. Something maybe to convince that brown-Crow teacher that I was just as well learned as her and she had no business keepin' me in that coop of a schoolroom and away from my business in helping Daddy and I hold Momma and Baby alive in our hearts.

Chapter 5

FED on FOOLISHNESS

On that first Monday morning of what was meant to be my purgatory, I half-expected to wake and find Daddy dozing with his rifle outside my window, my preferred shortcut for escaping trouble.

I whispered, "Trav, boy." Right away, he lifted his head, and his tail thumped the rag rug at its before-daylight volume. I wiggled my right pointing finger, and he went to the window and stood on his hind legs looking out.

The tail wag meant the coast was clear. "Good boy, Trav," and he went back to his rug to await further instructions.

"Trav, you figure Daddy's in the kitchen?" My stomach growled, and Trav lifted his head again, tail thumping out, "LET'S go EAT, eat, eat. LET'S go EAT, eat, eat." I obliged him.

But the kitchen was dark, stove cool. I looked out the back door, but no light came from Daddy's work shed. My stomach tightened up like a fist.

I went back to Momma and Daddy's room and

knocked on the door, which was ajar. It swung open, and the smooth white duvet in the dim looked like a snowbank. I made that bed myself every day, and I knew Daddy hadn't slept in it since I'd last tucked the corners and fluffed the pillow.

Trav whimpered, and his cold nose nuzzled the palm of my hand, which was still curved from knocking, but I wasn't hungry anymore. He padded back to the kitchen. When I heard his *whuff,* I pictured him settling onto his rug by the stove and followed him out.

I fetched water and stacked kindling by the stove, but still no Daddy appeared. I tried to act like it was a regular morning tending to certain chores, but I couldn't help seeing the dented tin pail that Daddy had set in the middle of the table the night before. That, I knew, was meant to hold my lunch for my first day of s—I gulped the word down without even letting myself think it.

Could Daddy have forgotten he'd sentenced me without trial? Or—? Maybe he felt so guilt-stricken he couldn't face sending me off to my doom.

Yet somehow I knew that wasn't it.

Beside the pail was one of the towels Momma embroidered from flour sacks. The way it was folded, three purple-thread crocuses grew out of the letters M-O-N-D-A-Y done in red and blue cross-stitch.

I traced the O with a fingertip and felt something hard underneath. A biscuit! Instead of lifting the towel, I traced the rest of the word. Felt like two biscuits. And I didn't have to look to know they'd be sliced open and smeared with bacon fat, which is about my favorite way to eat them.

I felt the scratchy heat behind my eyes that means you're downwind of your own campfire. I wanted to be angry that Daddy had betrayed Momma by agreeing to send me to school. I wanted to be angry he wasn't there for me to yell at him about it.

I wanted to go about my business and pretend I didn't know what was expected of me. I wanted to go out to Momma's tree and find her sitting there on her bench and put my head in her lap and have her run her fingers through my hair and trace my ears.

I wanted to be a million miles away.

Or to be ten again.

What I did instead, maybe because it was the easiest thing to do without thinking, was put that biscuit bundle in my pail, whistle for Trav, and head out to school.

Momma and Daddy met in school. But GrandNam said those two were too smart for school. I guess she was right since they quit and got married.

And I guess I was not too smart for school, because that's where I was headed.

The school itself was built on the far side of our holler, away from the woods and every good thing, so we had little occasion to be acquainted with it. After a piece, we joined up with the train tracks and followed them east as the mist lifted.

To me, the trains are like dragons passing through my kingdom, seeing me and mine, but paying us no never mind. I wondered if I would ever see the dragons' lairs, cities themselves loud and gritty, fast-moving and blind to what's around them.

You can put your hand on the tracks and tell if a train is coming long before you can see, smell, or hear it from the hum in that steel. I had set to know the rails' secrets as good as any Chinese worker who once toiled and maybe died laying down the line.

We turned off the tracks when we reached the junction box at the switch, and the sun was well up. From there, the tracks stretch on ahead straight and true before winding through the labyrinth of hollers and mountains.

I never yet seen a man or lady from China, but GrandNam told me stories, always reminding me that what the Lord made we had no need to fear. I would like to meet one someday and I'll be ready if I do. I'll tell him I walked his hard-laid tracks the only day of my life I went to school. Wouldn't take me more than a few hours to show that teacher lady that I'd already learned everything there was to know. I needed school about as badly as

Momma's sweet tea needed salt, 'cept of course when there were Crow Ladies nosin' around.

"School."

I didn't know I hadn't thought it till the word came out of my mouth, and it sounded loud against the crunch of my feet and Trav's snuffs and snorts. So we trudged onward, and whenever a thought tried to get into my head, I hummed something or other, torn between hating what was coming and loving what was now.

The woods don't lie or die or disappear without warning or make you do what you thought they had always promised to protect you from doing. Rabbits are always rabbits, and chipmunks are never raccoons, and a person could certainly learn a thing or two from that—like to avoid people and stick with animals. At least with critters a person knew they wouldn't be betrayed.

When Trav and I got over the last ridge, I was so thick in my own mud, it took me longer than a flash of lightning to realize that suddenly I was looking at my own sorrow mirrored in a familiar face.

What was wrong with Tully?

He sat above the last stretch of path, looking down on our place of confinement, and from where I stood, he seemed so still, I thought he might be hunting. But when I got closer I saw, although he was facing away from me, that he had no rifle nor flip, and so it seemed he was just thinking the rare but careful kind of thought that in Tully's case took all of his mind.

He jumped straight up when I tapped his shoulder.

Any other day, I'd have crowed at that.

When Tully finished gasping for breath, he laughed at his own foolishness, and I smiled at his open, familiar face. "You just stole one of my nine lives, Possum."

I laughed, but I knew what he was going to say next before he did and cut him off. "I promised Daddy I would give school a try, and that is what I am gonna do, Tully Spencer. I don't need a guardian to make sure I get there, if that is what you're here for."

Tully pulled back Trav's ears and said, "All I was gonna say is, they don't cotton to dogs in school. Even one as fine as Trav."

I felt skittery then. I knew the day would be short and that I'd have Tully there, but I hadn't figured on doing without Trav. What kind of school didn't let you even take your own dog with you?

Trav licked my hand and looked at me woefully, knowing my thoughts as he does.

"Don't worry, Trav." I scruffled his neck. "This won't take long anyway."

Tully spit out a wad of seed husks. "Know Newcomb's girl, Mary somethin'?"

"Some." I sat to pull a prickler from my right baby toe, pulling my foot real close to see what I was doing. Pressed around till I felt the sting. "Scrawny kid. Sniffly?" I recalled seeing her once or twice when I'd been to the store with Momma or Daddy. I spit on my foot and rubbed it to clean the spot. "Any time I seen her, she was holding a hankie over her nose like it might fall off otherwise."

Tully had his knife out and grabbed my foot, so I settled back, wriggling like Trav to feel the cool of the ground on my shoulder blades. "She sure did change some this summer," he said before spitting on his knife blade and digging the tip into my toe.

I closed my eyes, knowing I wouldn't squirm for something so puny.

"I went. Into the store for. Penny's worth of—"

"Ow!" I sat up and stuck my toe in my mouth.

"Sorry, Possum," Tully said, looking at it. He wiped the blade on his pants.

I scowled over my foot at him.

"Anyways, she shot up maybe a foot. Dressed up like a Sunday-school Christmas tree." He folded the knife and put it in his hip pocket.

My toe throbbed. The mention of Christmas made my belly swoon for the way it always had been, with Momma hanging greens from pillar and post till our house smelled like the piney woods, only better. But there'd be no such greening this year. Or ever. How could it even be Christmas if it wasn't the three of us like it had always been? Or four of us like it was supposed to be ever after?

Tully shrugged. "Anyways, reckon you'll see her soon enough."

What was he talking about? I looked him up and down. From the little pile of seed husks at his bare feet, he'd been waiting awhile. Did he come this way for me?

Truly a friend to beat all friends.

But wait. How did he know I'd be coming this way anyhow?

The sound of a clanging bell rose up to us on the clear morning air. Tully wiped his hands on his coveralls and pointed at Trav. "Best send him home now, Possum." At least he had the decency to sound mournful about it.

To Trav, he said, "Don't worry, boy. I'll make sure she don't get into no trouble." Trav woofed, and Tully hooted. "Unless I'm in on it too."

I knelt down and grabbed Trav's silky ears, rubbing my forehead against his. My eyes felt prickly. "Go, Trav. Go on."

He didn't budge. I swatted at him. "You gonna stay there all day?" He sat.

From below, the bell clanged again. Tully tugged my arm. "C'mon, Possum. Trav's more worried about you than you need to be about him." And I knew his words to be church-truth.

I let Tully pull me a few feet and turned. Trav barked once and then lay down, front paws crossed, chin on top. He was telling me he'd be there when I came back, no matter how long I was gone. That's when I remembered I wouldn't be gone long at all.

I reviewed my plan. Go to school, prove I already knew everything to be learned from Momma, and keep from wasting anyone's time or taking attention from the thick, slow, and unlucky who did not have a momma like mine to make school-schooling excessive. Then there'd be nothing keeping me away from Daddy. We could go back to pretending nothing had changed at all.

Sure in my plan of attack, knowing I'd at least have Tully on my side, I gulped hard and turned my back on Trav, marching onward like General Lee returning to Manassas.

My stomach growled about the breakfast it had not gotten. Maybe I'd wait till after lunch to leave school so as to not embarrass the teacher so much. I could have my biscuits to tide me over till suppertime. It promised to be the only good part of the day.

The schoolhouse was long and low, painted a rusty red with white trim, four windows along each side, its bell on a rail by the door. There was a tiny house nearly hidden behind it, which I knew had been built for a teacher to live in. Both buildings and the well between them lay in a clearing ringed by trees, with Hefty Rock to the back and the creek across the front.

When we crossed the bridge, our footsteps echoed down the water. I hoped the noise would wake a troll who would eat me so I wouldn't have to keep going, but we made it to the other side all right.

A tall, tidy woodpile stood by each building. I pointed and said to Tully, "You ever seen that lady pick up a ax? Cuz I don't guess she could lift one off the ground with two hands."

Tully snorted appreciatively. "Aw," he said, "lotsa fellas wanna help keep it stocked. Even Pa will send down a sled load come winter." Since Tully and his pa lived up in the hills, they got real good at using gravity to help 'em out. "'Sides, she's not so bad, I promise. Real smart. Smells good too."

It was my turn to snort.

Tully spit and grinned, but all he said was, "You'll see." And then, "You got ants in your pants?"

I was tugging at my underwear, which I had washed special, bluing and all. But drying them on the warming stove had made them stiff and scratchy.

I punched Tully's arm. "If this teacher's so smart, maybe she can tell how something blue makes clothes white." Tully scratched his head at that one.

The schoolyard was empty, but instead of feeling glad we had missed some of the foolishness,

I felt a speckle of regret at the idea that I'd be walking in like late to Sunday dinner. I was not for the first time in an hour glad I had Tully by my side.

We crossed the packed dirt yard, our steps slowing as we passed a split-log bench warming in the sun of the clearing and another settled in the shade of crooked pines. Any one of them would have been a fine place for Trav to wait for me, and I wished he was along. His black eyebrows made him seem wise, and I might have felt smarter having him nearby. But that was past. And this was the moment.

Tully and I stood on the step, and I took a deep breath, hand on the latch, before opening the door and stepping inside. As I drew the door closed behind me, the latch snapped like a hangman's noose and a dozen or so heads turned our way. I stood in the doorway and blinked a few times. Up front were some little kids I knew by sight, sitting to the side of what I took to be the teacher's desk. Bigger shapes, in shadow at the moment, seemed to shift in place toward the back.

On the teacher's desk were a jug of buttermilk, a tin of corn bread, two jars of preserves, a basket of eggs, a heaping pail of blueberries, and a mess of squashes, okra, beans, and collard greens. I heard my stomach rumble again but also felt embarrassed. How was I supposed to know people would take food?

Best thing would be to get out of there as quick as I could.

Most of the room seemed taken up with tables for two. Near a pull-down map of the United States, I saw a couple of the preacher's kids. It was hard to know which on account of they all look about the same. Plus they wore their straw hair in their eyes, which was a shame. As GrandNam said, eyes mirror the soul. Those children all had eyes blue as Heaven.

"Hey, Possum." From the back of the room came a familiar voice. Hoping to see a friendly face, I snuck a peek, but all I saw was coat hooks below a shelf of lunch pails. I set mine alongside for starters. I guessed them all to be filled with corn bread or biscuits, maybe a slice of cured beef or a boiled egg. My mouth watered, and my stomach grumbled.

Just then, I was nearly barreled over by a blur that turned out to be June May hugging me. A word for her is *excitable*.

"I'm real glad you're here, Possum," June May said. "Teacher's real nice."

"Back to your seat this instant, June May," came a voice that did not sound "real nice."

"That's not Teacher," June May whispered. "That's Mary Grace." June May scampered to her desk, just the same.

"Is that the Newcomb girl?" I asked Tully, but he had skulked off. Mary Grace stared, one fist on each hip, her mouth curved sour. Then, just as quickly, she smiled all innocent and sugar. She dropped a curtsy toward the opening door.

"Good morning, Miss Arthington."

Heads whipped toward the door, but my eyes were focused elsewhere. The light had hit a whole entire case of books in different colors and sizes. Books are not like schoolhouses. When you jump in, their pages open the world for learning far and wide. The kind of learning Momma and I craved. Like a brook trout that knows there's a hook in that dangling worm, I couldn't look away. There weren't the same old catalogs and stories I read over and over. These were real stories. My hands were itching like they'd been poison-oaked, and I figured they would keep itching till they'd touched each one.

In that moment, I forgot myself and would've gone right to them if Miss Arthington hadn't spoken.

"Welcome, *LizBetty*." Teacher's voice stuck on that word, and for a second, I thought it was Momma.

Then I felt my hair go up. "Don't call me that!"

The books faded behind rows of eyes, all darting between me and Teacher. Those eyes were set in familiar faces almost as clean as for church on Sundays. I felt like that trout, out of his pond. Trying to swim through dirt on the creek bank and finding it hard to breathe. It was worse than I thought. This weren't no place for learning; this was a place for judging. I felt that belly-churning like when you're gonna throw up, or worse, cry. I wanted to turn tail and run home to Daddy and Trav and Momma's pecan tree.

Chapter 6

KISS a FROG

"Back to your work, please, children," Miss Arthington said, brown gaze fixed on me.

Like one body with dozens of heads, everyone bent toward the table in front of them.

Except for Mary Grace. She stared at me, out from under a mountain of curly black hair, eyes green as pond scum. Arms folded, fists squeezed, she reminded me of nothing more than a solid tree trunk like our old oak only without the bark. Her lips, cracked and prunie, shaped a small, tight O that made me think of a chicken butt. But I've seen that look on the faces in Newcomb's or in church, and I knew what was the thinking behind it. The thinking was, I am better than having to be alongside something as measly as you.

She kept on staring at me like I might grow feathers, and I didn't like it one bit. You never stare into the eyes of a mountain cat 'less you want it to take you home for dinner. So I stared back at her and thought *SCAT* right at her as loud as I could think it.

Maybe she heard it, 'cause right then she looked down at her soft little hands and studied her pink tiny fingernails like they were jewels on a crown. A person who is not a pastor ought not to have fingernails so clean.

Teacher was still looking into me when she said, "Mary Grace Newcomb."

Mary Grace stood and spun like a beetle on its back and came to rest facing Teacher. "Ma'am?" She folded her pink hands in front of her.

"LizBetty, you will share a desk with Mary Grace. Mary Grace, you will make LizBetty welcome."

"MG," I whispered as I slid in beside her, "call me Possum."

She shook her head and pointed to the blackboard in front. In big letters in the middle it read, "Good morning, class." To the side, under "Welcome, New Pupil," was writ plain as day "LizBetty Porter."

The teacher continued. "Class, please give LizBetty the same reception you gave me, and I'd also like you to thank her father for bringing us such wonderful pine boards when you see him."

"My pa?" I squeaked like a mouse whose tail is caught in that mean cat's claw. I gritted my teeth and sat. I did not have a single word left in my head to swallow. Miss Arthington walked to the front of the room, where two dozen strips of wood were set neatly on the teacher's desk next to the pile of okra. I didn't have to touch them to know that they'd be sanded smooth as a baby's belly by my daddy and that lots of kids would go home tonight with something to do their sums on. My school-indentured servitude was as good as paid for.

As Miss Arthington gushed over the fineness of daddy's pine boards Miss Stupid Mary Grace dug her elbow under my rib. "Looks like Teacher might have a new beau," she whispered, all salt under the sugar on her breath. How dare she come up with such an outlandish notion. That thought made no more sense than gills on cats.

I squinted around the room to glare at anyone else who might have the same notion. But as my frown passed the picture of Mister President Hoover, it landed back on the bookcase that appeared to have three entire shelves of books. I got a notion in my page-turning finger that I intended to read every one. Seeing those books was like digging into a pork-chop breakfast after a night out trapping. I felt hungry to bite into them all. It was a feast, and I'd been starving too long. If it came to me being stuck in this class, at least Momma would approve of that. Surely, once Teacher figured out I knew everything worth knowing, she'd insist I take them home to read to Momma and Baby under the pecan tree.

"Miss Teacher," rang a silver-bell voice from a tiny girl up front near the windows.

The teacher leaned in alongside the girl and guided the small hand, murmuring. I took the chance to look around and get the lay of the land, not that I was planning to stay, but even a rabbit burrows from both ends. I needed to know what my choices were.

We seventeen students plus the teacher near about filled the tiny schoolhouse, twelve young'uns plus four big boys—including two of June May's brothers—and of course me. At least they'd have more elbow room come afternoon when I was long gone.

The boys—like me—wore their usual bib overalls, only cleaner than usual. The skirts of the girls' dresses moved around their knees as they turned to look at me, and the ripple of colors from their clean starched dresses made me think of butterflies. Only MG stood out in what was plain a dress from the Sears Roebuck, like as not.

I was relieved when Teacher handed out pencils and writing paper to begin. "Now," she said, "today we are going to study . . . the frog."

Frogs! I reckoned I knew about everything there was to know about frogs. That tadpokes start out like fishes that give up swimming, the way babies give up crawling when they learn the joys of jumping. That bullfrogs leave not footprints but belly and toe prints. That a frog always closes his eyes when he eats. Even where frog skin goes after they shed. (They eat it.)

I wished Daddy were here to see how worthless this school business was, as I had predicted. Still, I did have one question.

"Where do tadpokes' tails go when they fall off?" I asked. "Me and Tully have looked and looked and never found a one."

Teacher looked my way. Something about her expression made me go from feeling certain as snap peas to embarrassed, like I'd burped during grace in front of company. My feet steamed, and I yearned for cool grass under them to take out the fire. It was all I could do not to bolt for the door. Only reason I didn't is I heard Mary Grace Newcomb snicker.

Mary Grace raised her arm into the air. "Miss Arthington, that should be 'Tully and I.'"

Her and Tully what? I wondered.

The piglet continued to snort. Her tone, smug and scornful, put me in mind of a sassy cat teasing a poor, honest dog. "And also in addition, would you like me to explain to *LizBetty* that she ought-ten to face front and raise her hand and wait to be called on prior to beginning to talk?"

Miss Arthington looked between us. "Thank you, Mary Grace. I don't think that will be necessary."

Teacher turned to me. "LizBetty, I know you are

not yet familiar with our rules. Speaking out is not allowed."

Mary Grace sat and smiled like a fool.

"Yes'm," I mumbled. My nose tingled, like a foot does when you sit cross-legged too long.

"However," Teacher continued, looking directly at me, "we will begin by discussing frog eggs and tad*poles*. Perhaps you will find your answer in today's lesson."

I was surprised to be glad Mary Grace spoke. "I would *never* touch a frog; they cause warts. They're nasty."

From the back row came a low voice that cracked into a high one on the last word. "I think they're real tasty." Tully gave me that crookways grin that always settled me.

"Ew," squealed Mary Grace, turning four kinds of pink before settling on green.

I considered this curious behavior. Maybe those too-tight curls were making her simple.

"Very funny, Mister Spencer," Miss Arthington said. "Let's all have frogs for lunch tomorrow. Mary Grace, touching a frog does not produce warts— any more than kissing one will produce a prince."

"I'd rather kiss a frog than a Mary Grace Newcomb," I muttered.

I don't rightly feature why MG was acting so tartly, unless it was because until then she'd had a front row desk to herself. I suppose it didn't matter that I didn't want to be there any more than she wanted me there.

Still, for no wrong done to her I could own, she set on peck-peck-pecking at me.

For one, she stepped on my toes with her Buster Browns, which were shinier than wet rocks. She'd say, "Oh, I'm sorry!" like sorry was the last thing she might ever be.

For two, she drew an imaginary line down the middle of our table and pushed my things over if they crossed onto "her" side, which seemed bigger than mine and growing.

"You lost your senses," I whispered.

She squinted at me and smiled like a rattler.

For third, she was more trouble than rocks on Tuesday.

All told, it made for one of the longest mornings I could recall that did not involve a toothache or skunks.

At three-quarters past on the tick, Teacher said to take our lunches outside. "Fresh air helps the blood flow to your brains so you'll be alert for the rest of the day." I was practically out of my seat before her mouth was closed, that Mary Grace on my heels. She snickered as she whispered, "You need a lot more than that." Her elbow jabbed my side as she darted on past me.

"I can be fresh for you this second," I said, balling up a fist.

She slowed down and turned her smug-again face toward me. Then, barely looking away, she made a show of taking down the biggest, shiniest lunch pail. "Miss Arthington," she bleated loudly, "I brought candy to share with the class again."

Nobody could have been more pleased with their self if they'd a caught a mountain lion bare-handed and taught it to dance.

Teacher looked up from something she was reading. "That's very generous, Mary Grace. Class, please eat your lunch before having a treat, and be sure to thank Mary Grace for her thoughtfulness."

At that, most of the boys lit out for the door so fast they made their own breeze. I hustled on behind quick as I could to get myself a breath of freedom before I forgot how it smelled. But before I could get through the doorway, which was not big enough for a girl so full of airs, Mary Grace pushed past me without so much as a "may I." And right behind her, poor June May like to fall under that gal's wheels if she didn't calm back a mite.

Like a pageant princess, Mary Grace high stepped out onto the schoolyard, nose in the air, a flock of candy-lovin' hopefuls in her wake. To the nearest one, she remarked loud enough for all of us to hear, "That Possum is so immatured. I don't know how I'll survive a day. Still, a leopard can change its spots."

I snorted. "You're all stink and no skunk, Mary

Grace. Everyone knows spots are spots; they go all the way through." But she just kept walking.

Then, from a grassy spot about twenty paces away, lacy ankles crossed, Mary Grace rolled her swamp eyes in my direction. "It is a speak-easy-ism." She looked at the little kids around her. "It means to say something that means something else."

See what I mean? Dumb as the lacy pockets on her dress. All those little holes.

I settled by the creek to let its babble drown out the sound of that lacy lump. Even in that hot spell, the water made a quiet "come-here" sound, and I bet there were fish to be caught in the shade of the bridge and wished not for the first time that I had my cane pole. Close as it is to the hills, in spring this part of the creek is more stream and runs fast till long past the swimming hole.

I reached into my pocket for my whittling knife and rubbed my finger along the tear Momma mended last spring. I wished everything could be stitched back together so easy.

That thought put me in mind of June May and all those creatures she tries to save, even the ones you wouldn't think worth saving. A dose of June May would've done me good about then.

I hadn't even thought the period on the end of the sentence when she floated up alongside me and sat. From inside the neck of her dress she pulled the little pouch. Sometimes she strokes that bag likes it's a brown bird she's keeping warm against her neck, but other times she carefully takes out the penny, which she proceeded to do, and rubs one nail-bit thumb over Mister Lincoln. The look that comes over her then, you'd think she could trace her daddy's face on it, feel his whiskers even.

"June May, that penny won't be worth a cent if you rub Mister Lincoln's face clean off it." It wasn't the first time I've said it, and I didn't guess it'd be the last.

She said what she always says. "I kin feel his face smiling at me."

And I have to say that, despite myself, maybe because I needed a smile so bad, I smiled too, knowing that even in a world gone wrong, you could count on at least three things, so long as two of them were the sun waking in the east and June May thinking good thoughts.

She fixed those eyes of pale caramel on me the same way Trav does when he thinks I've said something wrong, and—putting a fresh tail on an old cat—said something new. "'Sides, it's not for spending, this penny."

I knew better than to ask what was the good of money you didn't plan to ever spend, which was just as well because right then Teacher rang the bell to go back inside.

I was doomed to give up another whole hour of my life to listen to Teacher read from a book called

"Paul the Peddler," and I didn't even have a penny to rub or a strop to chew. I envied June May her small comforts, thinking how nice it must be to be a sunny day in a calendar full of rain.

Still, as long as I was there, I thought I'd listen hard and be able to take that story home to tell Momma that night. At first, I thought it might be a sorrowful story, and I wasn't sure Momma would want to hear it. We don't like the sorrowful ones as much. But in the end, the story Teacher read proved to be about how hard work paid for itself in good ways.

Well, and wouldn't that be a nice life, if your name was Paul and you had stuff to sell and could make yourself rich.

I guess Teacher might've missed the point, 'cause even though she smiled when she finished reading and closed the book with one slim finger holding the spot, she asked us what the story was about. You could tell by that smile that she hoped someone could tell her. Not wanting to draw eyes to themselves, nobody said a word.

If she didn't even know what her own story was about, how could I be expected to learn anything between these four walls? Surely, this room was way too small to hold anything I didn't already know.

Finally, just to save the necks of all those heads hung low, I said, "Work hard and your life will be better for it."

"Miss Teacher!" whinnied Scary Grace, pushing down on the words as they left her mouth.

"Mary Grace?"

MG stood, smoothed her dress, turned to face the entire room, and said, "It is never allowed for students to speak without clear permission given by the *teacher*, this being the only way to maintain proper order and good manners in the student body."

It sounded like she was reading from a book only without the book. When she finished reciting, Mary Grace nodded her head like she had made a point. She looked at Teacher like a cat wanting thanks for leaving a mouse in your bed.

The teacher looked from me to Mary Grace and back.

I could not read her face.

"Please sit down, Miss Newcomb. Thank you." Teacher touched her collar at the neck and cleared her throat like she was thirsty.

"LizBetty, I don't want to have to remind you again against speaking out of turn. Why, what sort of society would it be if people just willy-nilly said and did whatever they pleased without concern for order, never mind the thoughts and feelings of others?"

Mary Grace raised her squashed piggy nose so high in the air I could have looked into her brain if she'd had one. As the teacher looked around the classroom for a moment, Mary Grace smiled with the side of her mouth nearest to me and elbowed me in the ribs again. "Now you're done for."

I took the teacher's words to mean this was one of the times I was supposed to answer, so I stood like I'd been told to earlier.

When the teacher looked my way, I said, "Ma'am, the kind of society where someone speaks out whenever he pleases would be a democracy."

Mary Grace stared long and cold at me, so I knew I'd finally gotten one right.

Still, my nose felt tingly again.

Teacher shook her head like Trav does when he has water in his ears, and I figured she would be about ready to send me on my smart way home, as it was clear as the creek that I was even smarter than her.

This time tomorrow, I'd be under the pecan tree where I belonged.

Chapter 7

THE HOME PLACE
and TOWN DAYS

I settled on the back stoop with rags and shoes. Spit and elbow grease do the job, Daddy says, and I like a reason to practice spitting as much as anyone might. For want of any trouble to get into, or anyone to blame it on if I did, I decided to polish up all the shoes in the house, which would be a grand total of four, or one pair each of mine and Daddy's. 'Sides, I did my best thinking when I was polishing shoes, and I had some important thinking to do.

I'd been to school for one entire week of days and was no better for it that I could see.

Only thing I could say for certain I'd learned was I could shave twenty minutes off the hour-long walk home if I climbed Hefty Rock and went around back.

That and that—apparently—some folks call a baby frog a tad*pole.*

I couldn't figure why Teacher hadn't told Daddy I was too clever for school after the very first day.

I was sure my smart pants were making the other students feel sore about their sad learning. When I tried to point these things out to Daddy, he said the matter wasn't up for discussion. Maybe he'd missed the lesson on democracy back when he was in school, or his head was just so full of Momma and Baby and the sorrow that there weren't no room left for reasonable thoughts. That's why I needed to be home taking care of his sad self. Every day we were apart, he seemed to droop more, like a seedling in parched earth thirsting for somethin' to keep it on growing.

Shaking the sad from my head, I twisted a rag tight around my knuckles. Having wasted the best piece of five precious days away from Daddy and the home place, I set to doing my chores as bigly and loud as I could to make sure Daddy noted what all was being neglected and how hard I was forced to work in the little time we had together. I was partway through fifty percent of Daddy's shoes when I felt his shadow on me.

"What's got into you?" Like he'd never before seen me do a lick of work.

"What do you mean, Daddy?" I made my eyes all big. That only lasted a second, though, because he was in the sun, so I gave him the sunshine salute and went back to my work.

He sighed real heavy and turned to leave again, so I blurted, "What say you and me go into town?"

He stopped like stone but didn't face me. "Possum, honey—"

"We need flour! And I been thinkin' about makin' Momma's apple pie."

Still he didn't turn.

Since Momma died, it seemed to me that me and Daddy about had got so we knew what the other was thinking. Still, it took me by surprise, Daddy practically ignoring me this way. It would have been a rare thing indeed, for he never could say no to me or Momma when it came to important things like ice cream socials and taffy pulls.

"Daddy?"

I'd decided I could forgive Daddy for sending me to school long enough to enjoy a market day. Every Saturday, when all the folks in these parts gather by the dirt lot just this side of town, it's like a church picnic. They swap sundries and stories. The smells alone can swoon a stone.

"I been hankerin' for apple pie for nigh on a week now," I said. "We can meander and keep an eye out for apples."

There are a whole lotta reasons to go to town depending on the sort of person you are. For most, it's as social as church, maybe more even, because the people with money in their pockets tend to be more interesting than the ones with sin in their hearts.

Daddy doesn't hold with gossip, and there's lots

of it goes on in this holler. Folks like each other so much, they seem to get into everybody else's business. But he is known for his woodcraft and has picked up supplies and sometimes even work by showing up in town. I hoped the thought of a job might lure him now. 'Sides, he enjoys talkin' a bit of politics now and again.

And the orange Nehi treat that came at the end. We always shared one for the walk home, an orange Nehi with three straws.

"I'm positively positive apples'll be right next to the Big Orange Nehi place, don't you think?"

"Quit worrying 'bout that sodee drink," Daddy said, but he broke a tiny smile so I knew he was agreed.

Thinking about orange soda all of a sudden made me mad for no reason, like a wasp gets. (Bees always have a reason; they're more civilized, I reckon.) I stamped a foot to try to shake the bitter-tonic feeling out of me. "Maybe I don't want any dumb old Nehi. And maybe I'll make a PEACH pie instead."

Daddy lifted his hat and scratched at his head. "Peach pie ain't near as tangy as apple."

Oh, for pity's sake, what does he mean peach ain't—

I looked up at him, and then we smiled for a blink, remembering the way we pretended with Momma to quarrel over what kind of pie nearly every week of every summer ever.

We took our usual path to town, passing where I'd break off to go to school, but I didn't see any need to bring up that old place on such a sunny day.

Seemed like Daddy and me on that path we three had taken so often before could walk it with our eyes closed, so surely we could share our memories without opening our mouths.

As the road wound lazy left, the carts and cars on Ferguson Field came into view.

Daddy said, "I got to see some people 'bout some things, and I guess you could use you a pair of proper shoes, now you got a proper teacher. I'll see you back here in an hour."

His face was open, but in a flash, I felt hot and slapped. He wasn't going to walk around with me like we used to with Momma? Why bother coming at all?

I reached for the closest mean thing. "How can you say that, Daddy? How can you stand so close to Momma's own footsteps and say she wasn't a proper teacher?"

His smile melted. His whole face seemed about a foot closer to his neck. "Possum, you, we both have to forget what we don't got and focus on what we do."

Wind roared in my ears, and one of those ugly toads jumped from my mouth, words I didn't know were there till they came out. "I know I can't be as good as Momma at anything, but it seems like you can't wait to make changes. Why, before you know it, it'll be like we never even had Momma."

I was running before Daddy could call "Wait!" but my feet couldn't stop if they wanted to. I tore down the road, my brain screaming what my mouth was trying to keep in.

Eventually it got shoved down into my feet. On the dirt road, they slapped out, "Come back, Momma. Come back, Momma." I wished I could just keep running till she heard me and did.

At last, my chest felt full of fire, like when I beat Tully for the breath-holding swimming-hole record two summers back. I slowed, then bent and put my hands on my knees while I caught my breath. Traveler, who had been at my heels the whole way, plopped under the shade of a tree by the side of the road, and I joined him.

"Did I ruin it for us, Trav?"

Much as we love trapping and frog gigging, me and Traveler loved going to town best—the way it used to be. Town days had their own music.

I'd wake early and eat breakfast and do my chores and sit on the stoop till Momma and Daddy were ready. I did what I could to help them along, asking useful questions like "Are you ready yet?" and "When are we going?" At first, every time I stood, Traveler got up too. Even the birds seemed excited, to judge by their flit and flicker. Usually, by the time Momma and Daddy were ready, the sun was full up and Traveler snoring.

On those trips into town, Momma and Daddy turtle-walked the whole three miles, holding hands, whisper-giggling. Trav and I ran off the road, exploring, and back, and off again, like playing tag and always having Home Free to come back to.

We'd follow where the dirt road rambled lazy left. Me and Trav crashed into thickets and hid behind trees. If I thought pirates lurked nearby, I only had to whisper, "Trav, 'ya, bo'," and he'd appear right by me. He and I were pups together, and we had our own language.

"Possum, you heard a word I said?"

Traveler tugged on one leg of my coveralls. Looking up, I squinted into a Daddy-shaped silhouette against a robin-egg sky.

"No, sir," I said. How long had I been sittin' that Daddy had time to catch me up?

Daddy's shadow spread and shrank along to the sound of a loud sigh. Then he turned and proceeded toward town once again.

He didn't say another thing, so neither did I. Still. I followed.

All I can reckon is that Daddy knew me well enough to know that me running away once was rarer than a blue moon and not about to happen twice in a row, much less twice in one day.

The second time that walk was longer than ever

with the weight of all that had been said—or not said. Yet somehow at last we arrived back at the noise and news, smells and sights of the market.

Market days bring together town folk, farmers, and country people like nothing else but a church social could. Everyone took the chance to trade or shop, bringing carts and packs full and leaving with them just as full. Plus, of course, everyone had to catch up on as much news as they could carry.

"Market looks to be bigger this time," Daddy said. "Folks done puttin' up summer gardens and crops are ready to barter out. Got anything in mind?" From where we stood, I could see jars of molasses, lumpy sacks of potatoes, bales of hay. The smell of fried chicken and fried catfish and fried who-knows-what all hung in the air. "Marbles, maybe." I wasn't sure if I was still mad at him.

"Again? You sure you wouldn't like you some toilet water or something else a young lady of your age should want?"

Who was that asking? Sun didn't seem *that* hot. "Dumb, frilly stuff? No, thank you."

"Lotta girls your age don't think it's dumb," he said.

Like he would know.

"Maybe a pretty little school dress?" He pointed the way we'd just come, and my eyes followed his point past a few tied-up saddle horses, two trucks, a car, and a buggy, all the way to—wouldn't you know?—that Mary Grace Newcomb, stepping from around the buggy and looking like she was drowned in pink snow.

"I ain't gonna walk around like no . . . ice cream sundee."

"What side of the bed you get up on this morning, girl?"

I ignored Daddy's question by focusing my ears on the sound of a wagon rattle-rolling over the hard-packed road somewhere behind me and trying to guess whose it was and whether it was coming or going. Behind and over the sound were others, people greeting and bickering, bartering, farewelling, and laughter, and—

"Hel-*lo* there, Lem."

Miz Pickerel! Last we'd seen of her, on church Sunday, she'd looked like any one of those old Crows that always seemed to be tormenting me and Daddy. But alone here, in a soft hat the color of June sky, she looked different. Kind of sparkly.

"How do, Miz Pickerel." Daddy smiled small but genuine.

How I loved that smile. And wanted it for just Momma and me.

"And Possum Porter. My, how you are growing! Are you and your daddy having a good time?" She sounded like she was cooing to a litter of kittens.

It was hardly the look or the voice she'd used in front of Miss Nagy on the day of the sweet tea rebellion. I blushed then, not so much at the thought of my little trick, but at the thought that Miz Pickerel might be thinking about it at the same time that I was thinking about it.

I shrugged and stared at the hem of her dark-striped dress. It looked to me like she'd wrapped herself in a preacher's tent. But forcing myself to look up at her, I had to admit that the color in her cheeks beat the cracked and powdered pale of most of the Town Ladies.

"Market's a little bigger this time, isn't it?" she asked, her voice then suggesting that it was Daddy, not me, who was the baby.

"Cannin' time," Daddy said, nodding. "I was jis' telling Possum it looked bigger. Don't you think so, sweetheart?"

I shrugged again. I couldn't believe I'd thought she was nice. 'Course, that was alongside the likes of Miss Nagy. At least Miz Pickerel's face wasn't as sour as old Miss Nagy's. But still.

"Did you see where they're selling apples?" he asked her. I perked, as I wanted to get apples for Daddy's surprise pie, even if I was a tad cross with him yet.

"Keep going, and you'll run right into them. Possum, you the one likes apples?"

Shoot! I didn't want anyone catching on to my plan, especially not her. I shrugged. My shoulders were getting their work done.

"Noralee made a fine pie," Daddy said, watching his feet as he shuffled up some dust. "We both of us miss that."

"Well, which one of you is the baker now?" Miz Pickerel asked gently.

Daddy smiled. "I was gonna take a hand at it. You know—"

"Why go to all that trouble? You're talking to the best apple-pie maker there is. Fine cobbler too."

"I don't want you to go to any—"

"Trouble? It's a pleasure." She was blinking her eyes like she had dust in them. "I'm fixing to bake tomorrow, and I won't hear another word against it."

"We sure appreciate you being so neighborly," Daddy said.

Was I hearing right? Did he just give away my job?

"Don't we, Possum?" He took my hand and squeezed it.

Sure, I appreciated having my Daddy's care and feeding taken from me and given to nearly complete strangers. I shrugged and took back my hand.

"I'm heading over to the rooster pen, picking me out a nice fryer. I don't suppose—"

"Good-bye, Miz Pickerel," I said, pushing Daddy away. "We got to go now."

"What's got into you?" he asked when we were a few feet and one mule-cart from that pie-baking devil.

"You wouldn't be visitin' and carryin' on so if Momma was here."

Daddy rubbed his eyes with one hand.

"You want me to forget about Momma?" I asked, fearing the answer even though I needed to hear it.

"Possum! Don't you ever say that again. You hurt me and you hurt yourself speaking such wickedness."

We passed washtubs full of Nehi and Co'Cola. My feet stopped like of their own accord, but Daddy kept on. "I'm not sure this is turnin' out to be a Nehi kind of day," he said.

And getting worse all the time, for coming up behind Daddy I saw Miss Arthington, all done up like a chocolate bar, but with brown flowers on her blouse. Aren't brown flowers the dead ones?

"Good afternoon, Mister Porter."

Daddy raised an eyebrow at me and put on a smile as he turned. "Hello there, Miss Cordelia."

"Miss Cordelia"? When did Daddy take to calling Teacher by her Christian name?

"Say hello, Possum." I managed the kind of wave that wouldn't scare a butterfly.

"We're makin' the rounds and runnin' into neighbors right and left," Daddy said. His voice was smooth, but I noted his eyes bouncing like rubber balls from me to her and back.

That was when I saw Miss Arthington signaling to Daddy, like trying to send him secret messages. Like if she thought I was a stump named Mary Grace instead of a person with eyes and sense.

"LizBetty," Teacher said of a sudden, "would you please get me a Coca-Cola?" She reached for the clasp on her handbag.

"Please, let me," Daddy said, digging into a pocket of his coveralls. Daddy was the handsomest man there. Still, I was glad to see he wore the ones patched on both knees, including the crooked one I'd re-sewed myself not long before.

Miss Arthington smiled. "If you'd like, bring three straws, and we can share."

I didn't know my face could burn hot and cold at the same time, with prickles in the tip of my nose and ears like they were on fire.

Daddy handed me five cents, still warm from his pocket, and they felt heavy as lead. I closed my hand around them.

I had no intention of getting a soda pop. I needed to get away. I shoved my fists deep into my pockets till I got to Guernsey's pig pen. I threw the pennies into the slop trough hard as I could. "Take that, and that, and that," I muttered, picturing Teacher's face on each bitter-odored coin.

Then I walked back toward Daddy and ducked behind a barrel of Bill's Pickles.

Daddy was leaning in toward Miss Arthington. Leaning in a bit too close, far as I could see. The breadth of Elliott County might have been close enough, to my mind.

I strained to hear.

"—so nice for school. How—?"

A commotion in the rooster pen drowned out Daddy's reply.

"A lady—pretty as a picture," Daddy said.

He thought she was pretty? That mushroom? I couldn't hear what Teacher said next.

Then Daddy said something about our house.

"Why don't I come by when she's not there?" Miss Arthington said. "She won't suspect." *That* I heard clear as church bells.

I expected Daddy to get red-faced mad and tell her to mind her own business and stay away. Instead he nodded. "After school," he said. "She and her dog usually take off into the woods till she gets hungry enough to come in. If you're sure it's no trouble, you could easily come by before she—"

Too much for me. I bolted, a dam full to bursting behind my eyes. I couldn't decide who I was madder at: Daddy for conspiring against me,

Momma for dying, or me for crying like a sissy. Again.

What I knew was I had to get away, and I didn't want to be found for a while. I went out to GrandNam and GrandPap's tree and sat in the clearing where nothing would grow. Every time I closed my eyes, I pictured things I didn't want to see, but at last I must've slept.

When I woke, I spotted Venus, first gal at the sky ball as usual. I lay on my back, hands laced behind my head, and looked up. I remembered something that, as usual, hadn't made any sense at the time. Like black night turns into mere dark once your eyes are used to it, memory shadows shaped themselves into understanding. Mary Grace was right. Daddy was courting Miss Arthington. Clearly, I had to get done with school as quickly as possible, if nothing else, to keep those two apart.

But at last I was cold and hungry enough to go home even though I didn't want to *be* home.

Home was supposed to be where people cared about each other. My daddy and his daddy built our house of rough-cut lumber. He taught me how they'd smoothed all the door casings and baseboards with a hand plane.

Since I could remember, whenever Daddy was bothered, he'd go to his shop and work a piece of wood, sometimes sanding for hours. Used to be I'd run my hands over some of his sweet-smelling wood, knowing the sweat and sadness he put into it. After Momma died, some wood got sanded down near to paper.

Usually, I loved the feeling of heading toward home, but on that evening, it felt about as familiar as watermelon in winter. The smell of sawdust and varnish reminded me only of what was missing, of what we had lost.

Watching Venus glide toward the horizon, I walked home by myself and was in bed well before she turned out her own lamp.

That night, instead of my usual post-town dreams about candy and show horses and distant friends, I dreamt about the day we buried Momma and Baby. Parts of it were like it really was, only nightmarish. Other parts were like cotton candy and not near so bad as the real thing.

In the dream, it was raining on people in our backyard. They were all huddled around Momma's pecan tree, next to the hole that would be her final resting place. Inside the hole was the box Daddy made. Inside the box, only we couldn't see them, was Momma, with Baby in her arms, wrapped in a clean flour sack. Preacher's mouth moved, but there was no sound in my dream, not raindrops on pecan leaves or hymns or my screams, which were tied up inside my head and throat and stomach like some long, twisted, wet sheet making all the pain wind together till it hurt in my teeth.

Trav wasn't allowed at the ceremony, so I leaned into the man at my side. He was old, almost thirty, the handsomest and saddest man there. He put a hand on my back, and the coffin was lowered into the ground, as if his touch made it go down, even though I could see the men working the ropes.

I held a small bouquet of wildflowers and dropped them onto the coffin. What I wanted was to drop myself and go with them to wherever God had in mind. It must be pretty there, not raining, and we'd all be together, the three of us. I could get to know my little brother. But I knew I needed to look after Daddy. It's what everyone kept saying, and it's what I promised.

My sleeping self watched my dream self close her eyes and shudder. Then I woke on the floor, Trav licking my face.

I climbed back into bed and did the same thing I had just watched myself do at the end of the dream. I took my sorrow, all wet and raw like a chew bone straight from Traveler's mouth, and buried it deep inside myself. I closed my eyes and shuddered. Then I tried to forget where I put it.

After that I fell back asleep and dreamt nothing.

Chapter 8

CRIED a RIVER

The Monday after market weekend dawned stormy and gray, which also happened to be about exactly how Daddy was acting. I never thought I'd rather be at school, but I wasn't about to stay where the air was full of electricity and angriness, even if the alternative was a dose of that human castor oil, Mary Grace Newcomb. At least if I was at school I could keep an eye on Miss Teacher too and know she wasn't anywhere near my daddy.

'Sides, at school I enjoyed the scratch of pencils and the squeaks of wooden desks, and I liked to watch the chalk dust swim through sun patches. Of course, it was interesting to talk trapping with one of the Justice boys at lunchtime or win a few marbles from Conrad Harris after school. And it was never too soon to see Tully again, even if we'd been out the night before frog gigging till midnight. Even the mix of smells from lunch pails and wood smoke was a welcome change from the nothingness smell of a house without Momma.

Matter of fact, if it hadn't been for Trav, I might just as soon have been at school reading *Heidi* or *Just So Stories* from Miss Arthington's shelf as go home to the empty house. Daddy seemed to spend every waking blink in his shop. And if he was in the house when I got home, as often as not, he'd make some excuse and leave till after dark.

But I was going to fix all that. I had to. I was going to find a way to stay home with Daddy and fix up our lives as best I could. Before he started to forget about Momma. Before Miss Arthington wiggled her scrawny self between us, trying to fill a hole in our hearts that couldn't be filled.

'Cause even with home being less and less like home, I did not look forward to being pestered by the likes of Mary Grace Newcomb. Every day began with the "Pledge of Legions" said to the flag of our country, which hung in a corner, and grief from that girl.

We were sat together I guess because we are about the same age, give or take a lick of sense. And as soon as a day started, I felt like I'd been there forever.

"Something stinks," she whinnied, soon as I sat. She made a face like an apple core and pinched her porky nose with two pink fingers. "My momma would never let me outta the house smellin' like you."

The clock being on the back wall made it hard

to know how long I'd be stuck alongside her. I was clean enough to pass Daddy's inspection, so I couldn't figure. "Must be you," I whispered back. I began to understand why an animal in a trap might chew off its own leg.

Then I remembered, the day before, me and June May found an interesting tree trunk, which we suspected of being rich in honey. We smoked out the bees from one end and took home two pails full of combs. 'Course, raw onion rubbed on is the best cure for bee stings, so maybe I did have a whiff of something about me.

I was about to explain all this to Mary Grace when she trod my foot. Right then I decided to bring fresh-cut onion to school daily. Maybe one in each pocket.

Nor did I enjoy this kind of distraction. If I had to be at school, I planned to show this teacher how Momma had already taught me everything worth knowing.

I just wanted to first see how things worked, which is about the best kind of learning a person can have. Daddy taught me to watch on top of the water to know where the fish whistle underneath. Far as I know, my daddy never didn't catch a fish he wanted.

Already I could see Miss Arthington had a system. Some kids sat in front getting lessons; everyone else sat to the back and studied quiet till it was their turn. I liked to watch the bigger kids using what they called flash cards to help the littler ones with sums.

All the day, Miss Arthington taught about English and geography and arithmetic and history. After we played outside, we sang together. It wouldn't have been too terrible, if I hadn't known that every day I spent at school pushed me further away from Daddy and the life we built together, us and Momma and Baby.

"You sure were in fine voice today on 'The Old Gray Mare,'" Tully said with a snicker.

I snorted. "I tried to be loud enough to cover *someone*, I'm not saying who, who sounded like a sack of cats being drowned."

But I could not drown out when Mary Grace ran on all day answering Miss Arthington's questions.

Even if they weren't directed to her.

Even if they weren't questions.

Even if she didn't know the answers.

As I told Tully more than once, Mary Grace talked pure to hear her own voice, not that it was special.

"Aww, I dunno, Possum. She seems awright, I reckon."

"Please, her voice sounds like it's been covered in molasses on purpose. Mostly it comes out real sl-o-ow, then sometimes it shoots out faster and spikier than the quills on a porcupine." Tully just shook his head and said nothing, because what was there to say when faced with the sad truth?

When Miss Arthington asked about the second president and Mary Grace started on about how Thomas Jefferson was her great-great-great-great-so-and-so's something or other, I was ready to smack the girl just for breathing.

Instead, I raised my hand.

It was that or explode.

Miss Arthington "called on me," which is what they say, even though it's not visiting. I stood like I'd seen the others do. In my saying-prayers voice, I said: "The second president of the United States was John Adams."

Teacher looked like she'd just eaten something GrandNam made. Mary Grace Newcomb looked like she'd just eaten something Traveler made, and I sat down feeling like pie.

"Now, students, if I may please have everyone's attention?" Teacher clapped twice. "Pencils down please. Face front, hands folded, feet on the floor."

When it sounded like everyone had settled, Miss Arthington said, "I have an announcement."

Mary Grace primped her curls, like one had to do with the other. Then she went stock-still, staring at Miss Teacher. Or rather, at what Miss Teacher held.

"Class," said the teacher in a hen-scratchy voice. "I am pleased to announce that this beautifully illustrated book of fairy tales will be the prize in an essay contest."

It might have been a trick of the sun that the edges of the pages looked covered in gold—or it might have been another sign from Momma. Maybe she worked this out with God to make up for me having to be at school.

"Now, it's not brand-new, but it was well cared for by a girl I knew who loved to have adventures. And she had many, in her mind, by reading these stories."

I felt my insides swoop like blue jays and heard myself give a sharp in-breath. Mary Grace looked my way, so I crossed my eyes and stuck out my tongue.

"Don't that girl want to go on 'ventures no more?" asked Connie. Then he stood, and said, "Sorrydon't thatgirlwanttogoon'venturesanymoresorryandthank youmiss," and then sat down again real fast.

Instead of getting angry, Teacher smiled. "You know, the thing about stories is that once you read them, really read them, they stay with you for always and always, and maybe you don't even need the book anymore but can share it with other children who want to have adventures of their own. Children like you."

The teacher continued. "Sometime between now and parents' night, each of you will write an essay."

"What will we write about, miss?" asked one of

those blond preacher's kids, maybe Ruth. She might have been the one played the lamb in last year's Nativity.

"Excellent question, Ruth," replied the teacher. "I would like you to write on someone important to you. The student whose work this term shows the most improvement will receive this book as the prize."

It came to me all in a flash. Write the essay, win the prize, prove once and for all to everyone— Daddy, the biddies, Miss Teacher, Scary Face Mary Grace—that Momma was right and the learnin' she gave me is a far-sight better than any teachin' I could get. Not even Miss Nagy could argue with a prize that included golden-edged pages.

After that, everything would return to normal. Or as near to normal as we could get without Momma. Daddy would forget all about his secret with Miss Arthington 'cause he'd have me to take care of him.

Some of the class murmured. Conrad Harris groaned out loud and earned a look from Teacher for it. Mary Grace licked her lips like some kind of lowly beast, some kind they would not have let into the manger when Baby Jesus was born.

Mary Grace picked up her pencil and wrote: "Essay, Imp person. FAIRY TALES!!!" The words *fairy tales* were underlined three times.

She was in for a sad shock. I pictured myself

under Momma's pecan tree, reading to her and Baby. I wasn't about to let a prissy little Kewpie doll take what was rightly meant to be mine.

Mary Grace cupped one hand over her paper and wrote something else.

"I'll leave this book up here to inspire you all," Miss Arthington said, placing the lovely thing on her desk. "The essays also will be judged on how well you follow the topic and your use of language. I look forward to seeing what you come up with," Miss Arthington said. "I know you will make me proud."

Mary Grace shoved the paper my way. She'd written: "I'm going to win."

"That ogre on the cover looks just like you," I whispered.

Mary Grace Newcomb's hand again swished into the air.

I put on my innocent face from the nose up and covered my mouth with my hand. "My, what big ears you have." I threw in a pig snort for good measure.

On the schoolyard, away from Miss Arthington, Mary Grace got bolder than vinegar, talking about my hair and I don't know what all. Luckily for me, usually she stayed inside for the chance to polish Teacher's apple, but on that day, she had grabbed her dinner and practically skipped out.

I had my own bucket and went looking for food

and fellowship, as Preacher says. Unfortunately for me, Tully was still inside making right the sums he'd got wrong in the morning. But June May had to be around somewhere . . .

Wait a second. Was that June May talking with Mary Grace?

But no, here came June May toward me, grinning like a melon slice. Mary Grace must've been picking on her some, probably to get at me. I'd deal with Mary Grace later.

"My ma makes all my pretty dresses and petticoats," Mary Grace snorted loudly, twirling in the dirt near me. She was talking to the little girls, but I was sure she was doing it to bother me. I put my hand on the ear that had to suffer her most.

"Let's eat quick, June May. I got business with Tully."

June May put into her mouth a piece of corn bread that should not have fit and said, "You fixin' to win that marble he got from his cousin this summer?" Only it came out, "You fifinwn ftmrfle he grfms hscsfn fis summer?"

"You bet," I said, wiping a bit of her corn-bread spittle from my cheek. "Come see."

But as I stood, somebody poked me from behind. Hard. I spun around, fists in the air.

Mary Grace sang-song at me, "My ma curls my hair every day. I might get me a permanent wave next year."

Like I cared. "I'd give you a permanent wave good-bye if you'd *go* somewhere," I said back. Then I pinched her arm hard, and she kicked at my shins, but missed, before running away.

I set the rest of my lunch on the step and went over to Tully, who had just emerged from the schoolhouse and eaten his bread and butter before his feet left the porch. Nothing like a good game of marbles to put that fool girl out of my mind. In fact, for a while, I was blessedly unaware of where Mary Grace or June May or any of the kids had got to. I was hunkered down and about ready to whoop Tully and win away his prize cat's-eye.

Then from behind I heard, "Look at those wobbly biscuits!"

I turned to see Mary Grace pointing to where I'd left my lunch. "My biscuits are just fine," I said, "you ham." She was that pink. I swear.

I admit my biscuits weren't always as round as they were creative, but who was Mary Grace to throw stones? Especially when she ate pork and beans from a can, which I wouldn't feed to Traveler, just because her daddy took over the store and had fancy food to choose from on every shelf.

I was real sorry when Scottie lost the store and Mister Newcomb took over. I was sorrier once I knew Mister Newcomb had brought along this *dis*-Grace of nature.

I tried to ignore her and turned to Tully, who looked like he might cry, even though I was about to win that cat's-eye fair and square. What was the matter with *him*?

Suddenly, he hiccupped something fierce. "HI-I-I-C-IC-IC!"

'Course, it isn't sporting to play marbles when you've got hiccups, so we had to stop. What surprised me was it turned out Tully didn't know how to get rid of hiccups, and I had to stop everything right then and teach him. If I had a brother, this was the kind of thing he wouldn't have to learn out in the world somewhere but would already know, thanks to me, when he got there.

"What'm I s'posed to do?" Tully asked, like if I was queen of hiccups and all.

I tried not to roll my eyes; GrandNam said that was a sin even if it wasn't in the Bible and even if no one saw you do it. At times, Tully was too simple for his own good.

"Tell them to go away," I said. "Shoo," I added for double measure.

"Shoo," tried Tully, right behind me as usual. Then, "HIC."

Some kids laughed. Ruth and the little girls in a corner of the yard stopped their clapping games and came near.

"Remind those hiccups they are not welcome—never have been, never will be."

❧ III ☙

"You don't got no call t' HIC." He sounded like a sick toad.

"Put one hand on your waist and waggle a finger, like this." I demonstrated.

Conrad Harris and the middle-sized kids copied us. *Good*, I thought, *they're learning too.*

"It's rude to point," sneered Mary Grace from about six feet away, where I had not noticed her pretending not to notice us. She sniffed.

Tully looked from me to Mary Grace. On its way back around, his turning-red head HIC'ed again something fierce.

I'd had the worst town visit of my entire life. I had a daddy who seemed to have forgotten my momma and was trying to make me forget her too. I couldn't believe I had to put up with the likes of Mary Grace Newcomb on top of that, *and* I couldn't even finish a danged game of marbles in peace and quiet.

I ignored her with a long-suffering sigh and hoped Tully would do the same. To him, I said, "It's okay to waggle your finger at yourself, like in a mirror."

"But I ain't got no mir-HIC-ror, Possum," Tully said, sounding like a scared little kid, which made the real little kids giggle.

"Just pretend, Tully," I said. "'Magine it."

"I'll be your mirror, Tully," Mary Grace said. That daft girl curved her arms above her head like if she was a ballroom dance in a marathon.

I lost my concentration and spun on her. "MARY GRACE, YOU GOT MORE GABBLE THAN A GOBBLER."

Mary Grace turned another shade of pink and turned her back to me. She stepped away a few paces through the pack of my hiccup-lesson students.

"I know something else," Mary Grace chanted real loud. "I know somethin' REALLY GOOD, if anyone other than CERTAIN PEOPLE wants to hear it."

I looked over my shoulder at her and darned if she didn't have hold of half my crowd. "I know, and I'm gonna tell 'less'n that creature leaves me alone once and for all."

That girl passed gossip like cows pass gas. But I had no secrets from the likes of her, so I shrugged.

"LizBetty's daddy, Mister Porter, he's sweet on Teacher."

I heard that lion roar in my ears, and my eyesight went black around the edges. "Shut up!"

Mary Grace grinned. She knew she got me. "Your daddy's sweet on Teacher." She almost sang it.

"I said SHUT IT, Mary Grace." I tried looking away. The girls who played jump rope near the footbridge had stopped their twirling and hopping. The boys edged closer.

"Your daddy's a fool for love."

My head snapped back to her, and I sized her up. I was a mite small for almost twelve, and she was big for thirteen. I was an inch shorter but wiry and a *lot* stronger. My fists curled of their own volition.

"Possum!"

From far away I heard Tully's voice, like from the bottom of a well. I ducked my head.

"Possum! NO! Wait!"

That last word turned into a wail, then into the sound of the wind in my ears as I took a running start and rammed into Mary Grace something hard. She went "OOF" into the dirt, curls and all, and cried a river.

"Fight, fight," cried Conrad Harris, but it was over before it started, for there was no chance that priss was going to take a swing at me. I was breathing hard but none the worse except for a scrape on a knee where I'd landed after I bounced off her belly.

Ruth and some of the little girls had stopped their hopscotch and jump rope to help up Mary Grace and lead her into the schoolhouse, while a bunch of the boys came over and patted me on the back or shoulder.

I felt like a hero, but I still got talked to. Miss Arthington said next time she'd tell Daddy. I didn't want her talking to Daddy any more than she already had, so I promised to "be good," whatever that meant. To me, it meant winning the essay contest, leaving school for good, and putting nothing but miles between Miss Teacher and Daddy.

I didn't even snitch about what Mary Grace said, so she didn't get into trouble at all, even though I got a week of after-school chores.

I knew I couldn't let on, but it felt good to hit that girl. Fact is, the day you catch nothin' fishin' isn't the day you talk about later. I knew it was shameful to feel so prideful and spiteful, and I told it all at the pecan tree that night. I think Momma understood. I really do.

POSSUM'S ESSAY

By Possum Porter

Most evenings after Momma did the washing up, she'd go watch the night come. That's what she called it. Daddy would say, "Noralee, you're a crazy woman," but he said it real sweet and nice, and he made that bench for her just the same, didn't he?

Momma would smile soft and go out the screen, *thwack*, and the house breathed out, like when you fall and the wind knocks out of you. Wouldn't feel right again till Momma came back in.

When I was a baby, if I cried, GrandNam would hold me up to the screen and say, "Hush, now, Momma's just there, out on her bench."

When Momma died, the house breathed its last. And it never did feel right again, even though Momma is still just there.

Once, I asked Momma what she saw from her bench under the pecan tree. She looked up, like she could see the dimming sky right there in the kitchen sunlight, and smiled. She said, real serious, "Seeing the branches get dark, till you can't tell them from sky, is like watching God dye lace for a funeral."

Chapter 9

ONE TICK TOO FAR

When it was time to go home, Teacher reminded us, "I hope you all have been working on your essays for parents' night. If anyone would like to discuss his or her project, you may stay behind."

Mary Grace sucked her breath in across her teeth.

"LizBetty, please sit with your hands folded until I give you your first chores." It was the first day of my week-long punishment, doing chores after school.

One way school's like home is all the work to be done, and not just sums or book reports. The water pail has to be kept full with fresh, cold water from the pump in the yard. The floor needs sweeping, the blackboards washing, and the erasers beating. Wood doesn't just walk in on its own, any more than ashes from the stove carry themselves out.

Truth was, the work itself was no punishment—I'm strong and quick when I fix my mind to be. But all that quiet except for the sound of Miss Arthington's pen and the rhythm of the clock was a special kind of torture. It was funny to me how I never heard the pendulum swinging when the room was full of learning, but in those afternoon hours, it was like to drive me mad with tick-tocking and Miss Arthington's pen scratch-scratching along. It put me to thinking she might be writing secret notes to my Daddy, and the clock seemed to be counting down the minutes until she decided to ruin our lives forever.

On the last Friday of that punishment, Teacher finally said I could go. I ran for the door and freedom and Miss Eulah's place, for I needed to see her about a cure. Since none of my plans seemed to be working, it was time to consult someone with more experience in such matters.

I was past the creek, over the first fence, across the gully, and up the slope when I remembered I'd left my dinner bucket. Shoot! I was running low on time, and it was getting dark. But I knew I'd need my bucket come Monday, so I turned back quick.

Often as not, when I was kept after school for doing something that did not agree with Mary Grace, she would hang around like a noose and try to be useful, which was like asking a goat to say "please." Didn't she have anywhere to go?

But so far I was in luck. No sign of Mary Grace in the yard. I opened the schoolhouse door quietly, hoping to avoid any unnecessary conversations.

Right off, I saw Miss Arthington was alone, back

to the door. She was leaning on her desk. I saw her shoulders shake and thought she might be laughing at something on the floor. Then, from the sounds she made, I realized she was crying.

She wiped her cheek, and I saw a sheaf of pages in her hand. A letter! But who would be writing so to make her cry?

She didn't turn, so I guessed her own snuffly noises had kept her from hearing me. Quiet as catfish I backed out and closed the door.

On the steps was the last person I expected to see at school after hours. What was a shame-faced Tully doing sneakin' around there?

Tully turned red and ducked his head. I grabbed his shirt and pulled him toward the creek.

"What're you doing here?" I whispered.

"I ... um ... see ... lookin' for you?"

"Here I am, plain as your nose. And make it quick; I need to get to Miss Eulah's."

A shadow of what might have been worry crossed Tully's face. "You sick, Possum?"

Sick of Mary Grace.

But I shook my head. "Naw, I need to see her about something special, about a cure. I don't really wanna talk about it, but it's for Daddy, if you must know. It was something I couldn't even talk about with Momma, so I decided to go see Miss Eulah."

Tully motioned me behind the schoolhouse.

We sat at the base of Hefty Rock before I asked again.

"Whatcha lurkin' around here for?" I poked my jaw toward the schoolhouse. Usually, he kept his distance from school like it was a rattler pit—actually more, 'cause a rattler pit would be more interesting.

"Well, ya see." Tully wasn't much of a talker.

Usually, I knew what he was thinking and asked it for him, then went ahead and answered him too. But this time, I was stumped on top of perplexed. I needed more to go on. "Spit at the devil, Tully, and spit it out."

"Okay, okay." He swallowed and looked away. "I'm p—sh—M—eeg—s."

I breathed in. I rubbed my ears. I blinked my eyes. I wet my parched lips.

"What?!"

"I'mpartialtoMaryGrace."

Tully spit it out all at once like if it was rattler poison, but I was pretty sure I'd made out the words all right. Just in case, he said it again, slower, like he was getting used to the idea himself.

"I'm. Partial. To. Mary. Grace." Then he ducked, like I might punch him, which I might have, had I not been more stunned than a wild turkey beaned by my flip.

He was sweet on that, that...*useless* Mary Grace? I nearly fell over just with the thought of smacking him in the head.

He could have said almost anything—that he was giving up hunting or decided to become Conrad Harris's best friend. Anything. But—sweet on her? I thought I might be speechless. Though my speechlessness didn't last long. "That, that, prissy little know-it-all?"

I tried to recall if he'd knocked his skull harder than usual lately. "Why're you talking crazy? Look at me." I checked his eyes, and, no, they weren't shifty, although they did look a might red. "You get into the dandelion wine again?" I was noting his symptoms; maybe Miss Eulah'd have a cure for him too.

Suddenly, Tully gave what amounted to a sermon for him. "I want to make her like me. What can I do to make her like me?"

His lip quivered too much to be playing a joke. I knew when Tully was lying. This was something altogether new.

"Why don't you just poke me in the eye while you're at it, Tully Spencer? What for you askin' me what girls like?"

"I figured, with you being, you know, a girl— won't . . . you help me, Possum?"

"Tully. You. Mary Grace. That—no. No, I will not help you."

Would Miss Eulah have a cure for traitors? Or maybe a curse?

"Possum!" he bleated.

I couldn't decide if there was something wrong with his voice or my hearing. It seemed I might be losing my best friend on top of my momma, my daddy, and my Nehi treats. Why didn't he just take my dog and my flip, long as he was ripping my heart out?

Tully whimpered like a sick sheep. "How can I get her to like me, Possum? She's so . . . clean."

I figured Tully'd gone plumb loony. I sighed and squared my shoulders. Being as he was my best friend and might have a fever to boot, I reckoned I'd do my best to humor Tully. But if I was going to lose anything else I held dear, I'd see to it he did too. I felt a plan building in my head like autumn storm clouds.

"Why don't you give her something special, Tully? Something you really care about." All I knew was it should not be that green cat's-eye marble. I did not say this aloud, but I thought it real hard.

"You mean, like a present?"

"That's right, Tully, a present." I saw him furrow his forehead and let him stew on that for a while. "I know!" I said. "The rattler!"

That was one mighty fine snakeskin. I'd wished it mine plenty. It was a beauty. That's how I knew Tully was truly touched. Why else would he be willing to give up a two-footer?

"Guess I'll give it to Mary Grace at school

Monday," he said. "Think she'll like it, Possum, really?"

This was not the Tully I knew. I wondered where the real one'd got to. My Tully could field-skin a rabbit quicker than a person could pick up chiggers. He was almost perfect. But giving up his prize snakeskin?

Tully mistook my quiet.

"It's the best I got, Possum," he whined. "'Cept for my green cat's—"

"I reckon it'll do fine," I said quickly.

He didn't say anything.

I repeated, "I reckon it'll do."

He stared. I knew then that wasn't all he wanted. I considered my options. I didn't seem to have any. Finally, I bit. "What?" I asked. "Ya want something else, don'cha?"

Tully chewed on saw grass awhile. "I reckon this is asking a lot—"

I knew whatever it was, it would be. Church-truth, I was tired of his babble, and I reckon it showed, 'cause just then he blurted, "Would'ja give it to her for me?"

That did it.

"I believe, Tully, that girl's got you soft in the head."

Like GrandNam always said, *Eyes never know what God sees.*

"Possum, puh-lease?"

It was not pretty to see a boy the size of Tully beg like a baby bird. I would have liked to be anywhere except with that boy at that second. I'd heard about others acting the fool over women, but this was *Tully*. Usually, he was first to pitch jibes when others pitched woo.

Then he went one tick too far for scratching. "Well," he said, "if you're afraid . . ."

Huh! "Am not scared, Tully Spencer, so just take that back. 'Sides, I didn't say I wouldn't." Thinking, thinking. Aha! "I just wonder what you're gonna give me for it, is all."

Sometimes words jump out of my mouth like bullfrogs, without warning.

I almost felt sorry for him, about to give up two of his best treasures on the same day.

"Hand it over."

It's not that I wanted to take Tully's cat's-eye from him when he was plain feverish. I knew I'd win it from him soon enough.

"You know what I want."

He fished it out of his pocket, and I simply accepted it as just payment for this fool's errand on account of it seemed to make him feel better for me to take it. All along I figured, once Tully came to his senses, I could return the cat's-eye to him out of pity, then win it from him fair and square.

"Now leave me be. I need to get to Miss Eulah's and home."

"Possum!"

"Tully! This is an emergency with Daddy. I'll take care of your fool's errand tomorrow. I reckon that's soon enough to throw your life away. Just leave it at the place."

Tully nodded once and left his gaze on his feet. I tore off for Miss Eulah's. First Daddy, now Tully. Was there no stopping the changes once the first rotten apple had toppled off the barrel?

TULLY'S ESSAY

By Tully Spencer

A true friend helps you get what you want most.
Even if they don't want it too.
Even if they think you shouldn't want it.
Even if I have to give up a green cat's-eye for it.
That's Possum to me, a true friend.

I APPROACHED MISS EULAH'S FROM the south and was glad to see Conrad Harris's daddy had mown the meadow, which would have slowed me another five minutes. I didn't see Miss Eulah at first, as she was hunkered down working the dirt, her dress and skin and hat all about the same color as the rich soil. 'Course, I wasn't surprised when she lifted her head and said, "That Noralee's girl?"

"Yes'm, Miss Eulah," I said, grateful I hadn't startled her, for who knows what a shock could do to someone her age.

She nodded and looked at the sky, although I am sure she could not tell how dark it was. "'Spected you be here by now. We best hurry." She lifted herself to a standing position that was still more comma than exclamation mark. "Fetch me a cup of water," she said, and I dutifully went to fetch her a cup of cool pump water.

The first push of the pump was the hardest, and nothing came out. Miss Eulah smacked her broke-up lips and walked toward me in those tiny steps of hers. I pumped and pulled again, and a stream of rusty water came out in a rush into the trough below. I pumped-pulled a third time, and the water came out fast and clear, cascading in the last light.

Quick as a hummingbird, Miss Eulah grabbed the dented tin can from on top of the pump and filled it brimful without spilling a drop. She drank deep and then smacked her lips again and smiled as best she could with what teeth she had. She carelessly returned the empty tin to on top of the pump without any effort, and it remained balanced there improbably, like a waterbird on one foot on a green branch over a fast creek.

Then she nodded toward the steps to her porch. "See them flowers there?"

"The purple ones, Miss Eulah?" I didn't want to be rude, but it was getting late, and I hadn't come to chat about gardening.

"Ay, the purp. Look in one."

"Inside the flower? You mean inside the purple bud part?"

"Ay. See the snowflake inside there? Inside the purp?" she asked.

Amazingly, for they were so tiny, I did, once she told me what to look for. Maybe twenty "snow-flakes" ringed the inside of each purple bloom.

"And see inside the white, the yeller?" she asked as she climbed the porch steps. Dusty lowed quietly.

"I don't—wait, yes! I see the yellow. So tiny. That's amazing, Miss Eulah, but what I came about . . ."

She held up one wavery hand. "I know, I know. Here's what you need to do. You get them white flowers, only the white. Count them twenty times three. Drink in hot water the next three days. That fix you right up."

I stared at her. "But, Miss Eulah, it isn't me who's si—who needs help. It's Daddy."

She settled on her stool below the deepening-rose-colored udders. "Ay, child. You think you want a potion to help your daddy to keep things the way they were, but things are never the way they were the second they happen. The way we keep alive the people we love is by holding 'em inside. You fear you startin' to forget Noralee, sound of her, smell of those lavender sachets she put near everywhere. When you have love, you have memory, and when you have memory you have all the room you need for all the change you're gonna get."

"Yes, I—"

I chewed my lip to hold back my frustration. Miss Eulah had a cure for everything. Why wouldn't she help me and Daddy? "Sometimes talking is the best cure, child. Me 'n' Dusty listen if you got something to say."

I hesitated but then, as the twilight wound itself around the three of us, I spilled every seed of sorrow I'd been saving like it was grit 'n' grain for chickens.

I tore one of the precious purple buds at the neck, but Miss Eulah didn't say anything.

"Me and Daddy have about got so we know what the other is thinking. Don't need much talk, which is good, cuz Daddy isn't one for much."

I checked the bib pocket of my coveralls to see how many petals I had. I'd sort of lost count, but it was too dark to see for sure, so I kept plucking and talking.

"Sometimes I see him watch the sun dip behind the hills, like Momma used to do, and I know not to bother him, because that's his time to remember all the good we lost. Yet I swear at times he has nearly forgotten we ever even had a momma. He can be so cold. Though one time he called me Noralee, and I don't think he even noticed."

I wasn't sure how long I had been crying, or what I was crying for, but I could just hear the crickets and the *squirch, squirch* of milk on milk, and Miss Eulah humming something soothing, and at last I said the final terrible truth:

"I feel like every time he looks at me, Daddy sees Momma.

"I'd wish myself gone if he could have her back."

Chapter 10

PEAS for GHOSTS

Next day, having been to see Miss Eulah and drunk the first of my nasty cure, I knew I had to do my duty for Tully's sake and tried to make the best of it. As I whistled my way along the road into town, fingering the cat's-eye, I recalled all the times I'd walked that route when Scottie owned the store.

Scottie was sweet on GrandNam and gave me candy whenever we went shopping or a'callin', as GrandNam was like to call it. Turned out, though, Scottie was owed too much, on account of his heart let folks buy on credit when they had no money for his hand. That's what Daddy said.

So Scottie lost the store, and Mary Grace Newcomb's daddy took it over. I don't believe folks cared much for him, as he never gave credit or candy and seemed sweet on no one, not even Mary Grace, that part of which I can frankly understand.

Nope, nothin' was as good as it used to be.

I climbed the raised walkway that ran in front of the store and kept the mud from coming over the threshold whenever we had a storm that made the creeks run their banks. Worn smooth from so many customer feet over the years, I wasn't likely to get a splinter, and the planks, dark in afternoon shade, felt cool against my feet after the unseasonable hot dust of the road.

I walked in and blinked into the half-light, looking around like a noontime owl. "Halloo? Halloo?" Wasn't I about sounding like an owl too?

But no one seemed to be in the store, and since I didn't have any money, I didn't dawdle looking around. Having been there plenty when Scottie owned the place, I went around back, to where the Newcombs lived, behind and above the store.

Knock, knock. Nothing. I tried again.

"Come in," I heard faintly. Didn't sound like Mister Newcomb. "Is that you, Eleanor?"

I knew I was in the parlor, but the room was dark with night creeping into the corners, and I had to fix my eyes before I could make out a rocker by the cold fireplace.

Someone—or some thing—was in it.

If I were the fearful type, I reckon I would've thought it a spirit, she sitting there all pale and weird, dressed like in white frosting, rocking. I'm not scared of a thing, but that made me pucker up a bit.

Her gloved hands near her lap kept in motion all the time, like spring butterflies. "Eleanor?"

I stepped forward and swallowed. "No, ma'am. It's Possum Porter? Lem Porter's girl?" I figured this was Miz Newcomb, mother of Mary Grace and not one flea's ear's worth of what I expected. I could not take my eyes off her head, where a hat bloomed like wedding cake. Giant cabbage roses waved as I stepped closer. Finally, I tore my eyes away to look at her face. Her eyes were big as toadstools. "I'm sorry to trouble you, ma'am. Were you just now fixin' to go out? Because I can come back another . . ."

"Oh, no," she whispered. "I don't go out." She looked around the silent, dusty room, which was filled with too much furniture, all of it looking uncomfortable. Was this how Yankees lived? "They would never let me."

A couple of faded petals floated off the hat and settled around the hem of her skirts. I looked again at the hat, which she patted. "You admirin' my chapeau?" she asked.

I had no idea what a *shapo* was.

Miz Newcomb leaned in and lowered her voice. "Mrs. Roosevelt is coming to tea. But my hair, I never know what to do with it. Thank goodness for Paris fashion, *n'est pass*?"

I shifted my feet trying to think of something polite to say.

"Have you heard from Eleanor?" Miz Newcomb asked.

Going on gut, that toad hopping from my throat again, I spouted. "No, but did you know Miz Roosevelt was the teacher of our own teacher, Miss Arthington?"

"'No one can know all there is to know in the world.'" Her eyes and voice drifted like dandelion seeds before she noticed me again. "I wish I had shiny hair like yours!"

I was pretty sure my hair had at least a few foxtail stickers wove into it.

Her hands resumed their fluttering, and it came to me what it was. They moved like she was shelling; only you couldn't see peas, which seemed to be going into a bowl, only you couldn't see that either. Shelling peas for ghosts.

I shifted my feet, and my ears felt fuzzy. I never been around many spirits or crazy folk, so I wasn't sure how to act. I tried to remember if GrandNam had a rule for it, as she had a rule for most everything I ever knew plus a lot I hadn't gotten to when God called her.

Then I remembered the business I'd come for.

I held out the snakeskin. "This is for Mary Grace."

Miz Newcomb squinted confusion, then put back her polite face. "Aren't you sweet? What is it?"

That's when I thought maybe something had made her go simple. How else to explain not recognizing a rattleskin you're looking right at?

"Won't you stay? I'm sure Mrs. Roosevelt will be here shortly. Of course, it's a busy time for her. Franklin, Governor Roosevelt, is going to be president, you know."

Sure, I knew the election was coming November 8th. Teacher told us. I knew that Roosevelt fellow was governor of New York, where Teacher was from. I knew he wanted the three Rs—not "reading, 'riting, and 'rithmatic" but "relief, recovery, and reform." And I knew folks were tired of Mister President Hoover saying all the time that the worst was over, when each day seemed darker than the one before. Why, even Daddy was known to read the newspapers whenever he had call to be near one.

What I did not know is why one lady sitting in a rocker in the dark thought the wife of the next president of the United States might waltz in anytime for a cup of tea. Nothing Mary Grace had ever said about her momma made me picture this.

Before the flesh on the back of my neck had finished pickling, I had dropped the skin into her lap, and was out the screen door rounding the porch when I ran smack-plumb into Mary Grace. I believe it was the first time neither of us could find our tongues. I recovered mine first. "I was just leaving."

From inside the house came yelling. "Eleanor, thank you so much for bringing me such a sweet little gift. I shall name it Sunshine. I'll be so happy to celebrate your husband's election. You must bring him next time."

Mary Grace sputtered, "I can explain, I... she's..." I remembered who'd gotten me into this. Much as I wanted to dunk Tully in swamp water, I had promised my best friend and been duly paid for my task.

"Brotchoosumpin," I blurted. "From Tully." Then I took off. I wanted to see Scary Face's reaction but not as much as I wanted to be anywhere else.

Chapter 11

WHAT the COCK-A-DOODLE

Off a faint and narrow trail above the home place grew a perfect old tree that, about three feet off the ground, bent even with it, making a perfect throne.

"TRAV'ler!" I whistled for him to keep up.

From my perch, I could see all my world, the little valley and its costume changes, from bright spring green to golden summer to coppery fall. From that height, the world didn't even appear to be crumbling the way it felt. The air was crisp and clear and sparkled and glowed, brittle with weak sunlight but full of possibilities, of beginnings. Soon we'd know if we had a new president to take us all in a new direction. But even Mister Roosevelt wouldn't be able to fix the mess I was in. I'd been in school for near a month, and couldn't see an end in sight. I shivered. Might be some rain in the air too.

Momma loved the rain. She'd look toward the sky but shut her eyes, sniff, and say, "There's a change in the wind," and sure enough it would soon be raining. First rain after a dry spell was best. Momma would sit on the porch rocker and watch the drops bounce off the ground in a kind of wild dance. Sometimes she'd close her eyes and listen to the music with a Sunday-church face of joy and contentment.

"Change in the wind," I told Traveler, who joined me on the throne. "It's marchin' brisk and lively." Marchin' around me for sure. Maybe marchin' all the way to Washington. Wish it would stay up there and away from me.

I watched leaves dance and spin, and I wanted to go where they were going. I felt restless. If I sat too long, I got ideas I didn't want and thoughts I couldn't understand. Had to keep movin'.

Sure enough, before I was home, the rains came. I did my best to stay ahead of them, or at least dance between the drops. A fool's errand, as GrandNam might have said.

For the rest of Saturday, the rain fell in oceans; winds howled like dogs locked up during turkey dinner. The wet Sunday after I was certain I had ruined Tully's future with Mary Grace, he left a message for me. It was three rocks laid like a triangle, with a fourth balanced on top, and left in a certain place we both knew to check. That signal said to meet at our secret place the soonest I was able.

· · · · ·

I FIGURED TULLY WAS ABOUT to tell me he'd gotten over his crazy business and back to his regular old Tully self. My heart filled to bursting with the thought we'd soon again be friends made right. I even told Trav to stay where he was in front of the stove and keep dry, figurin' I could do without him for a few hours long as I had Tully.

I followed the fat, happy creek along, watching water jump to catch sunlight, wrapping its babble around twigs and rocks. I imagined the water boasted it was going places they—or I—never would. But I knew I would someday go places too, like the women Miss Arthington told us about, women like Clara Barton and Miz Eleanor Roosevelt and even Miss Arthington, who brought her Yankee self all the way here from New York just to teach the likes of us about the likes of them.

The creek might dry up to near nothing during the hottest days of summer and leave a rocky sand path past our tree, Tully's and mine. But now it was fall, the tree near-bare and the water rushing. I figured I'd find Tully on the big sturdy limb, about halfway up, holding the string to a trap we'd built. The string was tied to a stick that propped open the door. What we did was lay out bait, and when a muskrat wandered into the box, we pulled the string.

Muskrats, like so many of God's creatures, never look up. Long as the wind was with us, we could sometimes sit so long and quiet as to catch a pair in an afternoon, enough to feed both our families.

It was like that being with Tully, as comfortable and calm as muskrat trapping.

I followed the creek like usual, so when I rounded the last tree, I came to a full-on stop and nearly fell in. I couldn't believe what my eyes were seeing.

Behind the tree was an embankment, if you knew where to look. The tall oak with the swing had no lower branches, which made it perfect for keeping out busybodies. In the tree was our swing, which we kept tucked in the crook when not in use. Daddy made it for us from a smooth, sanded board and two thick ropes that filled our hands with little twiney splinters till Momma discovered what Daddy had done and gave us rags to cover the rope where you put your hands.

When you swung out over the embankment and the creek was full, like it was then, it felt like you were flying above treetops and oceans and the whole world. When I pumped my legs as hard as I could, that swing gave me a glorious feeling of flying, of freedom, of being able to go anywhere and do anything.

But on that day, I felt like the board had fallen away beneath me and dropped me cold into the creek. For as I approached what I saw was Tully sitting below our tree, staring up moon-eyed. And when I followed his gaze, what I found at the other end was that Mary Grace Newcomb, whose piggy legs were sticking out from my swing!

This was at least a double-triple betrayal.

I reached for my flip but didn't have it. Since I couldn't bean either one of them, and seemed struck dumb to boot, I sat and just stared.

Next thing I knew, a friendly breeze helped me hear some of what they were saying. Some folks might consider that eavesdropping, excepting as it was *my* secret place and *my* best friend and *my* swing, I figured it was *my* right to hear any words that might drift about in these here vicinities.

Plain as her face, Mary Grace was talking dirt about me throwing a snakeskin at her ma.

Tully smiled all big like and asked her didn't she think it was fine.

I saw Mary Grace's face twitch like a billy goat's.

"Did—" She put her foot to the ground to stop the swing's sway, and I was pleased to notice her shoes were muddied up to her socks. "Did you have something to do with that...thing, Tully Spencer?"

Tully grinned like a brass band. "You don't get hold of a fine skin like that every day," he said proudly. "So ya liked it? Really truly?"

Mary Grace sputtered up a cough. "It sure is... differ'nt."

I could've given her credit for being slippery, but I didn't.

"I could pro'ly get you another, if you wanted," Tully said.

I wondered how he planned to do that. Maybe off Mary Grace's own backside. The snake.

"No!" Mary Grace shouted. Then quieter, "No, thank you, Tully Spencer. I do believe one present from you is just about the right number." She smiled at him like a sick calf. She fluffed her black curls. She blinked at him like she had dirt in those scum-green eyes of hers.

And Tully looked like pulled taffy.

I don't know why I'd thought Tully would see through that shabby pantomime—maybe he'd been bit by a wild dog.

Then he did the unthinkable, the unforgivable. He pushed her on the swing, and—I almost fell over—he commenced to singing. "I've told every little star / Just how sweet I think you are / Why haven't you I told you? / Da-dumb, da-da-da-da-da-da-dum, da-dum-dum, dummy—"

Actually, he sounded more like a bull moose in rutting season. And I was pretty sure he had most of the words—and notes—wrong.

I hightailed it, scheming the whole while for something fitting to get back at Mary Grace, but nothing seemed terrible enough compared to stealing a person's best friend and their swing and their Secret Spot, all in one rain-soaked afternoon.

I wouldn't have thought it possible, but Tully

had given everything away. Showed how little he thought of me. I felt like dirt on a worm belly, only worse.

Were all boys and men so shallow and gullible? It occurred to me then, out of the blue, only the day was gray, that Jump Justice being a mature age fourteen would never treat a person like Tully was treating me or like Daddy was treating the memory of Momma. I was sure of it.

Suddenly, I knew just where I wanted to be. I'd ask Jump for advice. He'd taught me how to tie a horsefly once. Maybe he could help now, especially with Tully, who seemed an equally knotty mystery. I swayed my hips and patted my hair pretending I had piggy curls as I watched my reflection in the creek. Was there something Momma hadn't told me? Hips bouncing and giggle-simpering. But Momma had never done such silly nonsense. Still, I wondered what it was all about. Persons with common sense, the like of Daddy and Tully, turning all to mushy rotted potatoes over such silly lady stuff as bobbed hairs and lacey dresses.

Next thing I knew, I found myself coming up on the Justices' place. And wouldn't you know, like if wishing could make it so, that once I had it in my head that I was looking for Jump, that's when I ran into him. I mean, *smack-crash* into him, though he looked no worse for it.

"Jarvis, you maggot milker!" he barked at me.

I was flat on my back in the mud. When I sat up, I saw stars, and Jump saw me.

"Possum Porter? You ain't Jarvis. You awright?" He reached out a strong, tan hand and took mine, easily pulling me from the mud, which released me with a *thwuck*.

"'Course I'm all right," I said, mentally checking for broken bones. "You?"

"'Course *I am*," he said. "'S'you I was worried 'bout."

"Worried, really?" I looked at him looking at me and suddenly remembered to take back my hand, which I quickly wiped uselessly on my now muddy coveralls.

"Not worried-worried, I mean—What the cock-a-doodle you runnin' from anyway?"

That bristled me. "Why you think I'm running from a thing, Jumper Justice? I ain't afeared a nut-hin'." I pulled myself to my full height, despite sinking a little into the mud.

Jump scowled. "Then how'd my milk get to be a mud shake?"

I looked at the ground. Sure enough, a battered tin pail lay at my feet, traces of white bubbling into fresh wet tracks. "Oh!" I bent to pick up the pail. So did Jump.

Crack!

We straightened, each rubbing a forehead. I could feel a knot building.

"Cricket spit, Possum. You okay?"

"I said I was, didn't I?" I summoned what dignity I could. "If you could just tell me where I could find June May . . ."

Jump grinned and pointed to the house. "Reckon you can make it without hurtin' yourself?"

My face felt hot with pique, and I spun on my heel. That was when I tripped on the pail and fell face-first into the mud.

When I got up, Jump was nowhere to be seen. At least he had that much sense.

JUMP'S ESSAY

By Jump(er) Justice

I reckon a fella don't need more'n a rifle and a knife and a lick a sense to git along in this world.

If I was pa to my own kids, like I feel to my brothers and sister since my pa went on the road, I guess I'd want a gal like my ma, what could shoot and skin and run fast and not mind getting wet or dirty and to make your supper.

If you didn't have one, I guess a blue tick would be about as good, and keep you warm, and not talk back neither.

I RAN INTO THE MUD ROOM off the kitchen and saw June May with her nose near the table, doing some sort of figuring. I let my teeth, which were beginning to chatter, announce me. Near right away the eyes in the back of her head told Miz Justice to turn from the counter, and she saw me dripping there.

"Possum," said June May, looking up. "How come you're all muddy?"

Without a word to me, Miz Justice sent the twins for well water. Then she took me by the shoulders toward the stove. "Peel off those clothes before you catch your death."

"Possum, Possum." June May was singing my name and skipping around and around the table.

I recalled one time those twins—Jessup and Jarvis—got sick real bad. GrandNam took over the home remedy and didn't leave till the boys were safe and well. Miz Justice said GrandNam was an Angel of Mercy.

That's what I thought of when Miz Justice held up the big crazy quilt for me to wash behind. A definite snap hung in the air. I wrapped myself in the quilt, and Miz Justice gave me a quick hug. I felt her hard belly up against me and remembered Momma doing that same thing. I coughed out the sob building in my throat.

"Possum, Possum," June May sang again, settling into her chair like a wild bird that might take off again any moment.

"Hush, girl," Miz Justice said to her, and to me, "Hot drink now."

While the kettle spit, it shook quietly. When it whistled, Miz Justice gave me hot water with honeycomb to take out the chill, and while I sipped, she took a rag to my face and hands to get off some of the worst mud.

June May had simmered down and settled deep into whatever she was working on, which she was being real secret about. Miz Justice shooed out the boys, who'd come back in to goggle, and let me set awhile before she asked, "You all right, Possum?"

I didn't know what to say, because I didn't feel all right. Church-truth, I felt all wrong.

Like she could read my mind, Miz Justice scooped me up and squeezed me until I thought I wouldn't ever breathe again. "Lordy," she said, "if Noralee could see you now," and though it sounded like she was laughing, when she let me be, she looked weepy-eyed. She must have been chopping onions, only I didn't see any around. Then she went out to rinse my coveralls.

I sat by the warming stove thinking June May had forgotten me when she raised her nose an inch from her schoolwork, scratching on a bit of wooden tablet Daddy had given her from his own shop.

"Possum," she said suddenly, "what kind of candy you think would that Miz President Rosebelt like?"

I was relieved this odd question had nothing to do with my mud bath. "Why would you ask a thing like that, June May?"

June May thought an awful lot about candy. When Scottie had the store, me and June May would sometimes go and look at the rainbow-colored jars behind the counter. Well, I looked; June May studied. She even moved her lips like Conrad Harris did when he was reading.

On paydays, when Mister Justice settled his store account, Scottie would give him a sack of candy and say, "You keep them boys as sweet as June May now, y'hear?"

Once, June May told me that if she ever had a nickel for a whole sack of candy, she would get string licorice. I personally prefer caramels because they last so long.

"Why licorice?" I asked. "It's not even your favorite."

Those well-deep June May eyes turned onto me. "Licorice fits the most in a bag," she whispered. "Caramels have those paper tails on either side that take up room in the sack, but they don't even have any *candy* in that part." That was June May's way. Now she said, "Because if she came to call, Miz Rosebelt, I'd want to know what kind of candy to serve."

I shook from my ears any mud that might be left. I'd nearly forgotten my own question.

But by then she'd tucked back into her school-work.

In the all-but-scratching quiet, I almost felt like falling asleep. As I shifted on the little stool under the quilt, I smelled myself drying and caught what I thought was a whiff of sawdust and sweat, the scent of Daddy coming in after a day spent in his work-shop. I felt my stomach wrench to think on him.

"Possum," she asked after a few minutes. "What's a pre-dator?"

"How's that, June May?"

"This word. P-r-e-d-a-t-o-r."

I thought a minute. "Oh, predator. That's some-thing that goes after something weaker than itself, like a fox is a predator to a hare. Some predators," I added, "when they ain't real hungry are just plain mean, like that nasty barn cat of yours. I seen him corner a mouse, let it go, then corner it again. Poor mouse don't know he's good as dead." That got my mind to swirlin'. Was Tully the cat or the mouse when it came to Mary Grace? My thoughts smacked up against each other; Mary Grace sure could be nasty as that barn cat. Maybe she was just toyin' with Tully? Or maybe I was the mouse and they were all toyin' with me.

And suddenly everything came spilling out, about Tully and Mary Grace and the snakeskin and Jump.

"Ooh, I could just smack him!" I fumed, recalling it all.

"Which one?" asked June May. "Tully or Jump? Or Mary Grace?"

"Both!" I said. "All three, maybe!"

I heard what I thought was a chuckle and noticed Miz Justice had come in, but it seemed she was only coughing.

June May shook her head solemnly. "I got enough brothers," she said, "I reckon I know good as anybody how boys are plain funny."

I reminded her we'd never seen any of those brothers—not even Jump in the mud just now—act loony as an outhouse mouse, as Tully seemed to be.

"Maybe Tully's sick," June May suggested. "Could he've been bit by a wild dog?"

I told her I thought we'd've heard. "I don't understand what's going on," I continued as Miz Justice added hot water to my cup. "Tully's gone funny. Daddy's being contrary. Now even Jump's gone moony-loony asking a person if they're all right all the time? And I can't control any of 'em like I used to. What's happenin' to everybody?"

Miz Justice sat at the table by us. She looked a little sad but real pretty in the kitchen light. I realized how much of the time she was worried, because right then, for a minute, her face was smooth as river rocks. "Did you girls know that you can't know what a fella is thinkin', or feelin', by what he says or even by what he does?" she asked.

I snorted. "What's the use in that?" I figured I could talk honest to her, since she was Momma's best friend.

Miz Justice looked thoughtful, turning from me to June May and back. "You girls know how, if a dog gets too close to the nest, the momma quail will go limping off, tricking the dog away to keep the babies safe?"

"Sure." I nodded. I'd seen it myself once when Trav burst into a thick hedgerow and scared out a fat quail. She flew off before he could get too close, but not before she'd led him down and around away from that nest.

"Well," said Miz Justice, "sometimes boys are like quail. They pretend one thing but are really feeling something else."

"I don't understand," said June May. "Does Jump have a secret nest?"

"I don't want Tully's eggs," I added.

Miz Justice laughed and rubbed my damp head. "I shore wish Noralee was here," she said. "I bet you do too, huh, Possum?"

She combed out my tangles, and it didn't even hurt, just like how Momma knew how to do it. "For now, let's say this. If you girls see any boys acting funny, ask yourself, is there any kind of fox nearby they might be acting funny on account of? Because when a fella's sweet on a girl, sometimes he does foolish things."

Chapter 12

PIQUED as CREAM

Even while I slept I knew rain drummed on the house like fingers waiting for something to happen. And the day loomed like me—steely gray and cloudy. Like I was stuck in a tangle of blackberry canes, every way I turned thorny thoughts dug deeper...Boys and daddies talkin' stupid or not talkin' at all. I knew for one thing certain I did not want to face Daddy...I had already decided to skip breakfast, but I didn't have to worry because as I woke he was leaving to help fill sandbags in case the river rose more. Four years ago, Miss Eulah's porch ended up in a field near six miles from town.

I knew for a second thing certain that I didn't want to run into any people whose initials were T. S. or M. G. N. (meaning Tully Spencer or Mary Grace Newcomb), so I lit out like home from church—fast and light—more to keep from thinking than to beat the rain. When I got to the main road, I took one of my secret paths, planning to scoot over Hefty

Rock and shimmy down into the yard behind the schoolhouse.

I had to drop the last four feet, but I knew the ground would be soft from all the rain. Sure as shooting, halfway to school the rain began again, bringing up a smell of earth to fool you into thinking it was a thawing spring day—only this rain was made of drops little and sharp, not the fat, lazy ones of spring. I moved into a trot.

At the rock, I bent my knees and dropped, rolling when I hit with a squelch. My flip flew out of the bib of my coveralls.

When I looked up, wasn't I looking—again—into the face of Jump Justice?

Jump grinned at me; upside down it looked like a sad-clown mouth. "You flat on your back in mud again, Possum Porter?" he asked. Then he disappeared from my line of sight. This was getting to be a habit. And a bad one at that.

As I got my wind, I felt the seat of my pants soak through and sat up. My head felt light and my heart thumpy.

That's when I saw Jump waving my flip above his head. I held out my hand for it, but he flaunted it like a trophy, so I could not reach it for leaping. Jump grinned while he played keep-away.

"Come on 'n' get your old flip," he drawled at me.

Before I knew it, Jump had led me to the side

of the schoolhouse, where we startled ourselves by startling two other people.

My brain barely had space to register them. Mary Grace Newcomb and June May Justice? What could Mary Grace be doing to get her rooster spurs into June May? I gave her an evil-eye curse that GrandNam learned once from a real Gypsy.

At the same time, Jump yelled to June May, "Git along now afore I git you along."

Why, they hadn't even done anything wrong, at least, not yet, far as I could see.

Still, both girls skedaddled.

I was tempted to follow, but I needed my flip before I could take care of Mary Grace or see to June May.

And at that moment, Jump was leaning against the schoolhouse, grinning and waving my flip around above his cowlick.

Next off, everything happened so I wasn't sure of it, even later.

Time slowed as Jump leaned down toward me. He smelled sweet, like fresh hay and sunshine, in spite of the sputtering rain.

And then, well, he kissed me on the cheek. Toad's truth!

His lips were soft and warm like rising dough, and it didn't feel wet like a dog kiss or anything like I thought it might.

I was thinking all these thoughts at once, so that

it took me a minute to realize I should be piqued as cream. I held stock-still. A storm roared in my head, so I barely heard Miss Arthington ring the bell.

Jump gave me a crooked smile and a wink and put my flip into the bib of *his* coveralls. Then he slipped past me, and I got another whiff of that sweet hay smell that made me think of warm summer days, far away from this cool, gray one. He strolled into the schoolhouse whistling "Dixie."

Finally, I snapped out of myself and drifted around the schoolhouse. The door was closed. I was glad no one could see me till I'd cooled my griddle.

When I walked in, Miss Arthington's speech revealed she was angry about something. "I've told you all time and again that I will not tolerate dangerous weapons in my classroom. I don't care if it's a twelve-guage shotgun or a pea shooter or anything in between. They do not belong in a house of learning."

Everyone else was silent and staring at the floor. I thought I might slip in without Miss Arthington noticing me, as her attention seemed focused on the biggest kids in the back corner, farthest from the door.

"I'm putting this in my desk, Jump Justice, until the end of the school year. And maybe without this kind of distraction we'll see more of you in school."

And what slid into that no-man's-land of her desk was—my flip!

Being flustered as flounder, I did not speak but tried willing Jump to look my way. Instead, he looked every way but mine, as a result of which I could see the back of his neck was red as rover.

As I had come in after the bell, when I tried to speak, Miss Arthington simply shushed me, which made Mary Grace giggle. It took all my willpower not to punch her. When I looked at Tully, he too-quick looked away.

"Where's June May?" Miss Arthington asked. She was looking at Jump. "I was certain I saw her before the bell."

June May's desk sure enough was empty.

"I honest don't know, Miss Teacher," Jump said. He seemed just as surprised to note she was not in her seat.

I was surprised at the quiet, inside voice Jump was using. He looked three sizes too big for the desk he was hunkered at.

"Honestly," Miss Arthington said.

I felt a flash of anger in defense of Jump. What'd he done wrong? Here he was being respectful and . . .

"You 'honestly don't know,'" Miss Arthington said, correcting Jump. "The adverb is 'honestly,' with an 'ly' on the end. It describes how. You honestly don't know."

When I realized Teacher was not picking on Jump, I switched my anger back to him.

"No, ma'am, I honestly don't."

I heard a titter and thought it might be Mary Grace, surprise, but she sat still as stone for a change, staring at her folded pink-piggy hands.

I shot her an especially extra-dirty look. She'd probably tried some dark sorcery to steal my other best friend from me, but she wasn't going to get away with it. If only I could get my flip back!

I already had lost one best friend, and, to make matters worse, Tully hadn't just deserted me; he seemed to have left the Confederacy and joined the enemy. June May was missing and who knew where or when that will-o'-the-wisp might turn up. Anyhoo, I couldn't very well tell her what Jump had done. Nor was I for certain turning to Daddy. Least not until I had won the essay contest and he'd figured out I was too smart to be a party to this gaggle of goose-brained idiots.

When I saw my flip disappear into the drawer of Miss Arthington's desk, church-truth, I had not felt so alone since Momma and Baby died.

Chapter 13

SURE as SHIRTTAILS

At lunch, the sky was dark as dusk. After school, though it was clear a storm was brewing, I hooked up with Trav and wandered the countryside, like maybe I could find the answers I was looking for hanging from some tree or sitting on some rock. It felt good to fight the wind, like it was cleaning me somehow. I found myself wishing again and again that I had a brother, a real live brother, I could talk to.

It was the first time I thought of him as someone who could've helped me, when all along I'd been thinking of all the kinds of things I would teach him. For one, he'd be the best marble shooter in Elliott County. Not counting me.

For two, we'd've fished together down to the creek and, when he got older and wouldn't drown 'cause I'd taught him to swim, I'd take him to Silver Pines Pond. Probably at first I'd secretly hook a fish for him and hand him the pole, so he could think it was his catch. I figured you did things like that for little brothers.

And for third, I would've made him his own flip. With him and me being such great marble shooters, plus Momma's pecans, we'd never run out of ammo.

Wind painted the trees side to side instead of up and down, and I was near home when the first big, fat drops hit the dirt road. Then the skies opened up, and I was nearly upon it before from a flash of lightning I saw the bicycle by our front door. I folded myself into the wind and ran the last twenty yards.

Trav barked once at it, a sound barely covered by the rumble of thunder.

"Hush, boy. Keep quiet."

He put his maple-syrup-colored muzzle into my curved hand. With a lick and a cock of his head, he let me know he wasn't about to give away our position.

I knew sure as shirttails that Teacher had come to return my flip and apologize for the misunderstanding.

I wondered how long she'd been waiting and was glad to have let her stew a bit. 'Course I'd be gracious, but she had to learn. You didn't just go off half-cocked, jumping to conclusions before getting all the facts.

I ran inside along with about ten gallons of rainwater and stopped just inside the front door to let the water roll off my face. I was ready to accept all coming apologies, along with my flip, only to find Miss Arthington sitting in Momma's company chair and Daddy nowhere to be seen.

"Why, oh! Hello, LizBetty," she said, looking even more startled than she sounded. Then she raised her voice. "LizBetty, I was just talking with your father about—about the essay contest. Asking him whether you planned to enter. And also—also whether he could possibly help build us a lectern for the readings that day."

Daddy came in looking pink and sheepish. "Possum, what'choo doin' here?"

I felt a cold run down me. I realized right about then that I also was not likely going to get back my flip. "I reckon I still live here, don't I?"

"Well, of course you do, sugar. What I—"

"Anyway, me and Trav only came in to get something to chew on. I didn't know you'd be all busy. With a busybody." I whispered that last part.

Daddy's face turned colors like fall trees. "What did you say, young lady?"

I didn't fear Daddy would give me a lickin' right in front of Teacher. Still, I moved my way closer to the door. "I said, sir, I didn't know you had company, is all. I'll just be gettin' out of the way. I can see I'm not needed or wanted."

"You're going back out in the rain?" asked Miss Arthington in a voice so high it sounded strangled.

"Good weather for night crawlers, and we're already wet," I said, and me and Trav scooted before he could hang any more crimes on us.

It was Trav's idea what happened next, I swear. Maybe 'cause there's a little overhang on that side and the ground is higher. He went and sat under the window to the parlor. I tried to call him, but he just looked at me; then he lay down. I had grabbed him by the scruff when a soft laugh floated past the window. A laugh that belonged to none other than Teacher. She must have gotten wet when she was closing the window. But I could hear their voices hanging on the air, like laundry being pegged.

First Daddy's, low and warm, then hers, light and musical. I slid onto the ground against the house and listened like if my whole body was made of ears, but over the drumming rain, I could not make out but a few words each.

"... nice ... pretty ..." That was Daddy.

"... sweet ... simple ... my best ... so glad you ..." And her. Then, "... courting."

Courting?

She laughed again, and I heard Daddy's roasted chestnut of a chuckle, and the floorboards squeaked. Next came an unfamiliar humming of an unfamiliar tune, and I knew she was alone.

I shifted slowly to my knees and turned myself

toward the window slow and cautious, like a turtle changing direction. Then little by little I raised myself. Just as I cleared the sill, I heard Teacher's voice exclaim, "Oh, will you look at that!"

Found out, I dropped to the ground like a treed coon shot between the eyes. Twister winds blew in my head, and I ducked against the brunt of discovery.

Nothing happened.

I opened my eyes. Nothing.

I lifted my head. Nothing.

I unwrapped my arms from my bent-up legs.

Another laugh floated through the window, and I understood. I was not discovered. Trav panted a relieved smile at me.

I climbed back up to the window but off to the side and risked peering in. What was the worst that could happen?

I wished I hadn't asked myself, because I'd likely get answers aplenty.

But a month of carnival rides could not have shook me like what I saw. I crouch-ran away from the window, toward Momma's tree. But sick with the idea of facing her, I headed instead for the woods.

Trav followed at my side, and when we hit the tree line, we both broke into a dead run. I might have been trying to run out the scene in my head, but not even a hounded rabbit could run that fast.

What I had seen burned my eyelids so that even if I closed my eyes, the pictures wouldn't go away.

What I had just seen was unreal.

What I had just seen was Daddy holding a pretty little something of red paisley on yellow. Miss Arthington was holding up a dark green with mallards flying over it.

Even though her back was to the window, I didn't need to see more. That green had two blue pockets up front and a pretty blue collar, which I knew well.

I knew because these were two of my own sweet Momma's best and most favorite dresses, which she made herself. She cut the patterns from newspaper and imagination on our kitchen table. She sewed them herself with her own warm white hands. And when we went to Scotties for flour, she let me pick the flour sacks with the patterns I liked. I remembered those flying ducks. That red paisley might have been my favorite.

Momma only had but four or five dresses that kept any shape or color after all the wash-wear-work of her life, and she'd been buried in one. Here were two of the others.

I ran.

Daddy giving away what was left of Momma.

I ran.

And they laughed about it.

I couldn't run far enough fast enough.

Would Daddy see Momma or that venomous trickster of a teacher when she danced around with her bobby head protruding from my momma's best dresses? That couldn't happen. Daddy was for surely a right bit delirious with missing Momma, I could hold to that, but I couldn't deny what I'd known in the back of my thick skull for some time; my daddy was, sure as a snake bite, courting Miss Arthington somethin' fierce, and I had to stop it. Had to get out of that darn school so Teacher would have no business left to come dimpling her way into our lives!

LIZBETTY'S ESSAY

By LizBetty Porter

Momma died on a sunny Friday. Baby, who would have been Momma's only son if she had lived, and my only brother if he had lived, died the next day.

We buried them out back, near her pecan tree, where Traveler buried bones Momma wasn't supposed to give him, according to Daddy. Under the knobbiest tree, the one that Momma said had fingers like GrandNam's, only never when GrandNam was around to hear. And where Daddy had built a bench for Momma to sit and watch the night come, as she was given to regular.

Daddy used the wood from her bench to build the box for Momma, with Baby in her arms wrapped in a clean flour sack. Momma in her favorite dress, of polka dots she called Swiss.

While he built the box, he sweated and grunted and cursed, and after, he seemed more like Daddy, only not as solid, like one of GrandNam's soft old calicos gone ghost pale from years of clotheslines.

Daddy said there was no call to keep the tiny clothes Momma had sewed so carefully, out on her bench, under the pecans, in the final glow of those final days. He put the precious things in a biscuit tin I-don't-know-where and that was that. But he will always love Momma and me and Baby. So there. The end.

Chapter 14

A PRECIOUS THING

I didn't know things could get worse.

Guess I don't know everything.

When we next were at school, there was no teacher to ring us in.

Which was fine by me. I didn't know if I'd be able to look at her without all the hurt in my stomach spilling out of my mouth. But this time, my punishment wouldn't be after-school chores. Miss Arthington would tell Daddy all the terrible things I said. Maybe it'd scare her away from our broken family. Or maybe it'd just convince Daddy that I needed more "female influence" in my life. And then there'd be nothing to stop her from trying to turn me into no Yankee or sweep the smell of Momma from our house.

At last, several minutes after the clock showed who was tardy and who was not, Miss Arthington came into the room. All the boys' smart remarks withered on their lips to see her face. We knew, to a person, that something was terrible wrong.

Teacher looked like she had lost her best friend—and she didn't even *have* a dog. The room got so quiet you could hear time passing.

"Class." It came out a squeak, but no one dared laugh. She cleared her throat. "Class, something has happened that cuts me to the quick. I don't even know if I have the strength to tell you how . . . how betrayed I feel."

I turned barely toward Mary Grace, who was as attentioned as I was. Clearly she had no more idea what Miss Arthington was saying than a skunk knows about perfume.

"First off," Miss Arthington continued, "the essay contest is over. The prize, our wonderful prize, a precious thing, as all books are—"

Here she choked up, and I found myself leaning forward to catch what she might say next.

"The prize has been stolen!" She raised a hankie and dabbed at her red-rimmed eyes and pink-tipped nose. "I can only think that it was someone in this room who took it." Her face teetered between rage and hurt.

I had the uncomfortable feeling that Teacher was looking right at me, *into* me, the whole time she spoke. Maybe I hadn't been rightly polite when I found her sneaked into my house, but that didn't make me a thief. I wondered what kind of the scum that lives under pond scum would do such a terrible thing. Like we all hadn't lost enough already.

Then, right on the heels of that thought, I had another, one I almost regretted. Almost. That it served her right to be so upset. Here she was accusing someone of stealing some dumb old book when she was aiming to steal my daddy! I wasn't going to let her play on my sympathies, no, sir, so I gave her my best evil eye.

Teacher was sniffling again and fussing with a stack of papers—looked like letters—tied in a ribbon the color of tiger lilies. She looked up then but seemed to speak to the wall behind us: "When I think that I came all the way down here, turned my back on so much, because I thought I could make a difference." Then she seemed to turn her gaze onto each and every one of us in turn as she said, slowly, "Do you realize that I could be in New York City? And happy? And married?"

Then she burst into tears and ran out.

The class sat stock-still for what felt like a plum century—that is, if it went on any longer, we'd go plum crazy. Then everyone started mumbling and whispering. Sounded like a hornets' nest. An angry, excited, disturbed hornets' nest.

What troubled me was the gnawing feeling that Teacher really had been looking right at me. 'Course, I knew it was my imagination, because I never did touch that book, nor would I. It's what came next that made the thought turn like warm milk.

Mary Grace leaned over real close and whispered,

"You took it." Her breath was hot on me, and I felt my face catch fire from the words.

"What?"

"Miss Arthington knows you stole her book!"

I felt like I'd gotten a sucker punch to the gut. "You're crazy!" It was hard to breathe and think at the same time. "I didn't. And anyway, what might make her think something crazy-foolish like that?"

Mary Grace looked shamed-faced plus surprised. I started feeling like a treed coon.

"Well, um." She twisted a curl.

"Go on, Mary Grace." I hadn't known I could talk without one single muscle in my entire body.

That's when Miss Arthington, red-eyed, returned and sent us home. "I hope the person who did this terrible thing and took our precious book will have the decency and self-respect to come forward. The rest of you can go home; there will be no lessons today." She turned to face the wall.

A kind of quiet, happy-sad chaos erupted in the room, over which she yelled, "But be here all the earlier tomorrow."

I grabbed my new essay and tore it top to bottom and crosswise before letting the pieces float into the trash bin. Weren't even worth kindling. My heart pitted like a quarry stone to the bottom of my stomach. Whoever'd took that book had stole from me too. They'd taken my one chance to save my daddy from Miss Arthington's crow claws and get him back to thinkin' straight about who his family was, so he'd stop messin' everything up.

I glanced back at Teacher. Her sorrowful eyes lit right into mine, and she curled her finger, beckoning me to her. I had a mind to turn tail and shove free, but I knew she'd get a notion it was out of guilt. I let the rest of 'em tumble out the door and my feet shuffled forward, but not on account of me asking them to.

"LizBetty . . . Possum," she asked, all sputtery but not accusin'-like. "You know anything about the circumstance of our beautiful book missing?"

If she had a thought I knew about her takin' my momma's dresses, she might have a reason for thinking so, but anger licked through me like a stung bear covered in honey. I stood as straight and falsely polite as I'd seen Mary Grace. "No, ma'am. And I'm very sorry for someone to do such a thing . . . ma'am."

She nodded and turned back to starin' at the blank chalkboard.

I crept from the room stealthy as a fox from a chicken coop, not sure if she thought I'd done it, or just knew somethin' on account of the thoughts tic-tac-toein' across my face, even if she were reading them wrong. I did feel real bad about the missing book and mad about the dresses and right furious about her looking to snare my daddy like he was a rabbit with a broke leg.

On the schoolyard, everyone talked at once,

each with an idea about the book thief. Only Mary Grace, standing a few feet away, and I were silent.

I felt like every eye was an evil eye and every evil eye was on me, blaming. I looked around for June May or even that traitor Tully, wishing for some sort of friendly face, but saw neither hide nor hair of either.

I was sure Mary Grace had done something to that book, out of mean spite, just to turn Teacher against me makin' her think I took it. How else to explain the continuation of a world gone mad?

Mary Grace walked in my direction, but I didn't have the stomach to stomach her. I took off for the woods, not thinking too much about where I might be headed but of course ending up exactly where I needed to be. I found myself at the Secret Spot, which although it apparently had been renamed the Less-Than-Secret Spot for Traitors and Prisses, was blessedly empty.

I climbed into the Y of our tree to think and kicked our muskrat box to the ground. "Stupid Tully! Stupid Teacher! Stupid world!"

I grabbed my stubbed toes and was rubbing them right when my stinging eyes caught sight of something on the ground beside the battered muskrat trap, something I didn't recognize, wrapped in fabric and about the size of . . .

I knew it!

I jumped down from the tree right next to the

bundle, narrowly avoiding crushing the trap. Soon as I picked up the flour-sack bundle I could tell it was book-shaped and hefty. Sure enough, unwrapped, it was the book prize itself!

"That thief Mary Grace!"

I felt my fingertips numb and my face heat as I realized what she had done. Though I had blamed her in my mind, I hadn't really thought she could go earthworm low. Yet here was as much proof as pudding. I couldn't wait to take back the book to Miss Arthington and reveal Mary Grace for the fink she was.

I imagined Mary Grace being led away by the sheriff while everyone in town jeered and hooted, except of course for her crazy momma, who'd still be in her parlor waiting for Mrs. Roosevelt to not ever come to tea.

I pictured Teacher wrapping me in her arms, weeping with gratitude. "Oh, Possum, Possum. I'm so sorry I ever took Mary Grace's part over you. How could I have not seen through her character? Can you ever forgive me? Please, what can I do? Ask anything, and it's yours."

"Well, Miss Arthington," I'd say, spitting into the dust and raising my voice a little so all the folks of the holler could hear me, "I reckon there is one thing."

"Anything, anything at all, just say it, and it's yours."

"I reckon you could leave my daddy alone, is all."

A murmur goes up from the crowd, but it changes quickly to shouts and jeers. Miss Arthington nods once, then creeps away, her head hung low. Meanwhile, Miss Nagy leads the crowd in "Three cheers for Possum Porter, who saved our town from book thieves and man hunters!"

"Hip, hip, hooray! Hip, hip, hooray! Hip, hip—"

"I knew it. I KNEW IT WAS YOU!"

What the—? My head snapped out of myself.

There stood Mary Grace, hands on hips, like she just rode the Wells Fargo wagon into town. She looked sweaty and run hard, once-lacy once-white socks half-eaten by her shoes, but definitely triumphant.

"YOU SQUIRRELY GIRL! You knew you couldn't win the book fair and square so you just took it!"

"Me?" I ran at her, a whole life's worth of resentment steaming up inside me. "YOU stole it to make Teacher hate me and to make her shine on YOU! You're a stupid, fluffy bit of stinkweed! Crazy stinkweed," I added, knowing the word would right throw her like a flip.

We fought, kicking and scratching like tomcats, though she didn't even seem to know how to fight fair, or even fight, the priss. I pulled her curls, but still she wouldn't admit it. She kept saying I should admit it.

Mary Grace said, "Winning that dumb ol' competition over you was more important than any stupid book. I just want Tully to think I'm smarter than YOU. You and your big messy head."

Some notion about Tully started to sink into my head, and I let go of her stinking curl. Knowing how spiteful Mary Grace could be, well, it almost seemed truth possible beating me would be more important than winning the book.

I admitted that beating her was important, but that I also really wanted that book—but only if I won it fair and square. "Obviously, I had no good reason to steal it, which should be plain as pudding to anyone, even you, Mary Grace," I said.

The fight had run out of us, pulling our shoulders down as it ran out our dusty toes. Finally, I said, "If you didn't take it . . ."

"I didn't!"

"And I didn't take it . . ."

"So you say."

"Well, then, who did? 'N' how did it get here?"

Mary Grace and I both come to realize the truth in one struck moment eye to eye. We knew it weren't either of us for sure, and we knew exactly who it was. She near to fainted with this revelation. At the same time, we both managed, "Tully!"

Stunned, we sat hard and stared at each other again.

"But why would Tully take Teacher's book?" I wondered out loud.

Of course we both, in our own ways, cared about Tully, so our hearts were softened toward him.

We had to talk long and hard before we came up with what we figured might move Tully to pull such a dang fool stunt.

"It doesn't make any sense he'd want it for himself," I said. "He doesn't even like to read."

"And he's no thief," said Mary Grace, not that I think she'd know a thing about it, but she was right: He was no thief.

"But," I added, thinking out loud, "he knew I wanted that book bad."

Mary Grace looked at me for a full minute without saying a word. Probably some kind of record. "And he certainly knew that I was fixin' to git it for myself." She said this real slow and significant-like. "And maybe just so as you wouldn't have it."

"So he's my best friend . . ." I felt like I was doing sums in my head.

"And *he's my sweetheart* . . ." Again Mary Grace used that voice like what she was saying was so meaningful.

"And he for sure knew you and I were fightin' over it."

Mary Grace snapped her chubby pink fingers, making a pathetic sort of sound. "What if he, that is, Tully, what if Tully thought that by taking the book, we'd have—"

"We'd have nothing to fight over!" I saw it clear as baptism water.

Mary Grace nodded her curls into a dance. "He's so sweet; he probably thought if there was no contest 'n' no book to fight over, he could maybe get us to be'n . . . friends?"

"That sounds about right." I spit. "Ha! Shows how far off his rocker he's gone. Still, it's as good a reason as any I could come up with. It's so crazy, it might just be right. So what do we do now?"

A rustle from the bushes made us both jump higher than the cottontail that jumped out glaring at us like he was a squirrel and we were the nutty ones.

"If Tully's to blame, then we're both just as guilty for driving him to it," Mary Grace said, and I could see it cost her. I doubt that girl had ever felt guilty a day in her life. She grabbed the book and tucked it into the front of her pinafore.

"We've got to fix this for him," I said, having no idea how.

Mary Grace looked real serious in thought.

We were both of us realizing we'd have to work together if we wanted to save Tully from being misunderstood by everyone (especially Teacher). Tully's spirit flies true—maybe too fast for his sense to keep up sometimes—but there's no criminal-type dishonesty in his flesh or bones or the air he breathes.

Plus, though I didn't say so to Mary Grace, I needed that contest going again so I could win my book fair and square and get my plan back to chugging straight down the tracks to home and Daddy, once and for all.

I squinted in the direction of the schoolyard. "We've got to get out of here before he comes back. He'll come looking for me at the home place." I tasted how true that was as it came out of my mouth, but that didn't keep me from hearing the meaningful pause before Mary Grace said, "We can go to my house." She looked pained, but this was no time for her fragile constitution.

"Come on; I know a way no one's likely to see us."

Mary Grace grabbed at her skirt like that could keep a thousand stickers from burrowing in.

I felt a new-moon kind of faint smile tugging at my lips, but at the same time, I felt some sorry for her having so little notion of the world outside of walls. She could read every word in every book from now till Judgment Day and still not know half what Momma and Daddy taught me. Or what I would have taught Baby.

And just like that it came to me.

"We could write our own essay."

Mary Grace's face changed faster than a twister

tightening. "If we explain what he's done, and why"—she grabbed my arm and stopped both of us—"maybe he won't get into trouble."

I peeled her hand off my arm. "Maybe, maybe he won't get into *more* trouble," I sneered. "Can't you walk and think at the same time?" Behind me, I heard her huff, but in a moment, she was crashing through the underbrush like a wild pig.

Mary Grace's voice switched to her I-know-the-answer-and-I-don't-know-why-I'm-bothering-to-tell-you voice. "If I can explain that—that things are—are not always what they seem—"

Of course if she could do any two things at once, one of them was bound to be talking and the other was likely to be boasting. "If *we* can," I said over my shoulder.

"What?" She sounded cross, and I could hear her panting like Trav after a good chase.

"If *we* can explain. We. As in us. As in me and you. But I see what you're getting at." I was thinking fast to catch up to what she was getting at. "If you look at things one way, he was bad for taking the book."

Mary Grace chimed in: "But if you look at why he did it, it's really quite endearing. Sweet."

I stopped cold, and she walked into me. I could smell her mooney face start to mooning. I turned to look at her and spoke the word slow and plain. "D-u-m-b."

But I felt bad saying it. Which of us was a bigger heel, what called him dumb or what called him sweet? Plus, Mary Grace's bottom lip stuck out and started shaking like a leaf in autumn.

I sighed. "Dumb but sweet."

Chapter 15

SO MANY CHINA CUPS

Today the parlor curtains were pulled back and lamps turned on so I could see that Mary Grace's house was worlds different, worn to a shine with years of respectful using. Each family that had owned the store just passing through, borrowing it for a spell, like one of Miss Arthington's books. Not my house, built by my granddaddy and my daddy for real livin', and special just for us with chairs made comfy by lots of sittin'.

I could see the walls were whitewashed but no better to my eye than Momma's creek-mud ones, and the sofa was plumped up and covered in lacy bits—fancy dress clothes, as if to hide past scars and bruises, which're nobody's business even if a body can't help but look. Two matching armchairs with curlicued arms stood stiff like they were new off the Wells Fargo wagon, but dust and spider webs told different. I had to wonder the point in having such nice furniture if no one ever sits on it.

I dragged my pointing finger in a figure eight on

the arm of one of the chairs, the cool smooth of it like something too hard to have ever been a living tree. I raised my finger and sniffed it—lemony and talcum-powder sweet lingering smells of fancy city ladies. Maybe Miz Newcomb really had been shellin' for ghosts. I walked wide around the lamps with actual paintings on their bellies. They looked to be as fragile as Miz Newcomb's slender china cups, set out for tea, but never used.

But there were books. Books everywhere. Magazines and catalogs too but mostly stacks and stacks of books. Piled on tables, stacked on the floor, and even taking up space in a chair by the fireplace, across from the rocker where I'd found Miz Newcomb that day I delivered Tully's rattle-skin right into her lap. A lot of books had fancy letters on their covers with titles like *The Ancient Roman at Home* or *Adventure Under the Sea*. My fingers ached to touch them, and my eyes itched with wanting to read them. How could Mary Grace have all this treasure and be so blamed dumb? And these books, not like the chairs, had the look of being read and then some—the over-and-over kind of reading. It was a world of yet-to-be learning just asking.

I was puzzling the worth of furniture too fancy to serve its purpose when Mary Grace pointed to the chair catty-cornered to her at the big table of dark oak and told me to sit. She brought out paper and pencils on account that Miz Newcomb thought we were doing homework. She would flutter into the room every few minutes wearing a different hat. "Well, ladies, what do you think, is it right for tea with Eleanor?"

I had never seen so many china cups, 'specially without chinks, as were sitting on that table. She could have a dozen Eleanors show up and never run out.

Mary Grace frowned into her glass of lemonade, her lips cinched up so tight, you'd think the lemonade hadn't a bit of sugar in it. She slowly inhaled and blew her frown out through her nose. Now she just looked tired, and when she suddenly caught me staring at her, she rolled her eyes to the ceiling and back before turning to see her momma's newest imagining.

If only Miz Newcomb wasn't hanging all about us like mist on a bog. Finally, she exhausted herself and curled up on the parlor chaise like a calico cat and got to purring like one soon after.

"She won't wake up even if the house catches fire," Mary Grace said. "Don't know how someone can get themselves so tuckered out fussing about something that's only in her head."

"What's wrong with your momma?"

I tried to swallow the words, but they'd already hopped out like a bullheaded frog. I thought Mary Grace might start to cry, and I wished she'd just whack me upside the head for my stupid question. Which is what I'd a done to her if she asked about Baby and Momma.

We talked about the essay, what it should say and how we would sneak it back into school, but we talked about a mess of other things too, all civil-like, except she never did answer me about what had bent her momma.

WE SNUCK OUT OF THE HOUSE quiet as a kitten and headed back to the school.

"What we gonna do if someone's there?" Mary Grace asked, shifting the book under her dress, which did not bring ladylike to my mind, but sure made me grin.

"If we can't put it back today, then we better be there afore everyone tomorrow," I said. "Last thing I want is to get caught, especially with you."

An owl hooted. Mary Grace jumped out of her skin and right near into my arms.

"What was that?"

"A sea serpent," I said sagely.

Mary Grace did an about turn. "Let's take the book in the morning."

I scooted around so I was facing her. "But in the morning is when the Indians and bears are out."

"Oh, you," Mary Grace gruffed, turning toward school again. "How'd you get so brave anyway?"

"How'd you get so scaredy-cat?"

Mary Grace grew quiet. Too quiet. For her anyway. I figured she was troubled by some other foolish thing she'd done and needed to get it off her chest. "Something wrong, Mary Grace?"

"No-o-o," she said slowly. "Something's right."

"You got a funny way a-showin' it."

"I just wanted to say—"

We'd stopped walking. Her face looked like she was in pain, but her eyes were clear. She blurted, "Thank you!"

And like the levee bursted, she was her old self, blabbering like no one could stop her or should even try. "I really like it here. I got friends, 'n' Tully, 'n' Miss Arthington, 'n'"—she kicked the ground—"'n', well, you."

"Uh-huh," I said, but she didn't seem to need encouraging now.

"I'm getting used to everything, and I don't wanna move again, and it was so awful last time with all the whispers and doctors and all!"

Then I was lost. "Mary Grace?" But I might as well not have been there.

"It wasn't exactly like I said about how we come. It was dumb luck, gettin' Mister Scott's store and all. We really come to get away from the talk about Mother."

We walked on a mite farther.

"I wish you coulda seen Mother before, when

she was well," Mary Grace said. "She was so lovely. I was little, 'bout the size of that June May Justice, and she treated me like a doll. Made my clothes, fixed my hair, and taught me how." Mary Grace was nearly whispering.

I had to lean in to hear. "We always practiced on my doll babies. Now I have to do my own hair. Hers too—when she lets me."

What could I say to that? "Mary Grace, you got real bouncy hair, that's for true." I was thinking as fast as I could.

"Thank you, Possum Porter!" She looked pleased, so I guessed I'd said right.

Then she sighed. "I wish we could trade places."

"Why would you say a thing like that?" I asked, alarmed at the idea of those springs popping out of my head. How did she sleep even?

"Mother thinks I should act like a lady, that I should play in the house. I wouldn't mind being able to go around like you do." She took a deep breath and then let the next words rush out like a mountain spring: "I wish my ma was dead like yours."

"Mary Grace, that's horrible. You take that back right now 'fore I smack you."

Mary Grace took a step back and put up her hands, palms out, like that could protect her. "Listen. We left the last place because of her. We'll probably have to leave here because of her. She's more trouble than she's worth." Her voice was cold and flinty, like the back side of a boulder.

"At least you got a momma," I replied. "Any momma is better than no momma."

"Having a momma like mine is worse than none at all," she countered.

"Mary Grace, I'd give anything to have my momma back, even if she was loopier than sweet peas. I would, I swear."

"You think," Mary Grace said sagely. "But it's a burden. Especially on Father."

"Least your daddy can't run off and marry some teacher thinks you're a thief."

Mary Grace looked shamed for once. "I might of made up that part about your daddy being sweet on Miss Arthington. Fact is, she has a fancy in New York. His letters come to the store, and she writes him near ev'y day."

AN AWARD-WINNING ESSAY

By Miss Mary Grace Newcomb, Age 13

Even though some people say Mrs. Eleanor Roosevelt runs around the country without a man and how dare she poke her nose where she doesn't belong. And even though she is definitely ugly and homely and not nice-looking, she is kind of interesting. A person could see why another interesting lady, like our beautiful smart wonderful teacher, Miss Cordelia Jane Arthington, or my mother, Beatrice Orlene French Newcomb, might find her interesting. Someone might even want to invite the president's wife over for tea, and that would be highly respectable.

The End

MARY GRACE WAS FINALLY QUIET when we reached the school clearing other than when a spider scurried off the doorstep as I tried to open it quiet-like. We slipped the book and essay onto Miss Arthington's chair, then tiptoed out and hightailed it again.

I walked MG almost all the way back to her door. Grudging myself for goin' soft. As my feet made their own way down the path to home, I thought about Mary Grace and her momma. In some ways, she had really lost her mother too, except she could still smell her and hold her and that still seemed way better than talking to the damp cold ground.

And going the places Mary Grace had gone, living in so many towns. Yet she seemed as interested as a cat in a string that me and Trav never get lost in the woods.

I wouldn't care to say that I thought Mary Grace was pretty brave, always moving to new places with big buildings and or new people she didn't know from a litter of coons. And then again yet, she's scared of bugs with no stingers or pincers.

Far as I could see, that bundle of brindle alone made Mary Grace closer to interesting and not so crazy stupid after all.

Maybe Tully was right. Maybe if the two of us quit trying to slap each other to the ground, we might figure we weren't so different. Then again, maybe a magpie is just a magpie.

I asked Momma about it later, but if she had any answers for me, I couldn't hear them.

ALL THAT LONG NEXT DAY at school, I waited for a sign that Teacher had found the book or an announcement that the contest was on again. From the ants in her pants, I guessed Mary Grace was waiting just as hard.

At the same time, there seemed to be no evidence that Tully was in any (new) kind of trouble yet. For one, he seemed to be walking just fine, which told me he had not been whooped to within an inch of his life, which for sure would have happened if his pa had caught wind of what had gone on.

At the end of the day, Teacher asked Tully to stay behind. His face turned red and got twitchy like with poison ivy, but he would not look at me.

Mary Grace and I tried to take our sweet time leaving. For one thing, I hadn't told her, but I had decided to write my own essay anyway, on top of the one we wrote together. I didn't want Mary Grace to go off half-cocked and write her own dumb essay, so I was looking for a chance to leave it for Miss Teacher when Mary Grace wasn't looking. Thing is, she was hanging on me like a shadow. So I dawdled with my books at my desk, dropping this and that. Still, Mary Grace seemed even slower than excuses.

Finally, Miss Arthington shooed us to the door and out. Mary Grace said, "I got to get home, to, you know—"

"I'll stick around," I said, "see if anything interesting happens."

Not five minutes later Tully came outside. His face was still red, but he didn't look at all like he'd been whipped. He made one quick look at me, muttered, "Gotta get home," and took off running. I let him go.

The next day, Miss Arthington announced to the class that the essay contest was back on, with winners to be read at parents' night the following week. The room erupted in buzz.

Mary Grace elbowed me, and I kicked her under the desk, but we didn't look at each other. I was watching Teacher to see what she'd say next. Maybe we'd be heroes. 'Course, it was my idea, the essay . . .

Ruthie raised her hand.

"Yes, Ruth?"

"Does this mean you found the stolen book and caught the thief, ma'am?" Her voice was full of excitement bubbling over, like a fizzy drink you shake too much.

Miss Arthington smiled. She did not look our way; I am sure she did not. She simply said, "Let's say for now that I am feeling somewhat alleviated of my concerns of the past few days. I would prefer to say nothing more on the subject. Is that understood?"

A dozen stunned heads nodded slowly and said, "Yes, Miss Arthington." Then Conrad Harris raised his hand. "Miss Teacher, does this mean we won't never solve the mystery of the burgled book?"

"We will never solve."

Everyone groaned.

"No, class, listen," Miss Arthington repeated. "The question should be, 'Does this mean we will never solve the mystery of the burgled book?' I'm glad to see your visits to the matinees are paying off for you, Mister Harris."

Kids giggled, and he blushed. "Yes, ma'am. But will we never learn, you know?"

Again Miss Arthington gave us a secret kind of smile. "Let's say, perhaps more will be revealed."

Chapter 16

PRETTY *as a* NICKEL

On the night of the parents' program, I arrived early. I looked for faces I knew but didn't see Jump. Or June May. Or any other Justices. Or Tully.

I tried to quiet the bustle in my stomach by paying attention to things around me. The program was about to start when June May arrived and set the room whispering like wheat in wind. She led Miz Newcomb by the hand. Miz Newcomb made herself small but proper and sat in June May's little chair; June May sat cross-legged at her feet.

One look at Mary Grace up front, batting her eyes at all and sundry and primping those curls, told me she didn't know yet her loony momma was loose. I wondered what Mary Grace would do when she noticed.

I gave no thought to why June May was with Miz Newcomb. Maybe June May found her wandering and helped her in. June May had a knack for any living thing that wasn't right, probably didn't make any difference whether it was mind or spirit or body.

When Mary Grace went white as bedsheets, I knew she'd spotted her momma; of course, the girl was horrified. Her daddy must've been too because he suddenly materialized alongside his wife.

Crowds of parents, kids, and other relatives and townsfolk mingled, looking at the dioramas and drawings and maps placed all around the room. Most didn't seem to have noticed Miz Newcomb yet, but Mary Grace pressed her way through the crowd. Only God knew what kind of scene she might make if she got there first, and nobody deserved that, least of all Miss Arthington.

I had to head her off at the pass. Crunching toes, ducking elbows, I was able to grab Mary Grace by the back of her starch-stiff, navy-blue pinafore. "Psst!" I hissed, though no one could've heard us over the chatter of grown-ups.

Her eyes put me in mind of a trapped animal. "Leave me be, Possum. I need to get Mother home before someone sees her. Before she does something."

I took her hand and squeezed. "Mary Grace, you stay right here. Don't you care about Tully? We need to stay put and stay quiet and see if our plan worked."

At the sound of Tully's name, some of the

wildness left her eyes, but I kept hold of Mary Grace's hand as Miss Arthington called for attention. I was itching to know if my school days were over. If I had won, for surely I wouldn't need to be learning more stuff I didn't need to know. 'Cept my eyes kept slipping back to the beautiful books in the bookcase. Never mind, I thought. In a toad's leap I would have my own beautiful book.

I hate to say it, but I could not have been more surprised if Traveler had won the essay contest when Miss Arthington announced the winner. Of course, I was that proud too.

"I am so pleased with the results of our essay competition. As most of you no doubt know, the theme was 'an important person in my life.' And our prize is to go to the student I felt has shown the most improvement since the beginning of the school year."

It felt as if half of the room leaned forward slightly. My fingers were crushed white where Mary Grace squeezed them. Even the clock seemed to hold its tick-tock breath.

"Tonight I am proud and honored to announce that our great admiration—and this beautiful book of stories—go to . . . Miss June May Justice. Would you come forward, please?"

A buzz went around the room, with not a little clapping and a few squeals from the younger girls.

Ruthie ran to June May and grabbed her in a bear hug, beaming like she'd won herself and met the queen of England to boot.

I shot a look at Mary Grace. She appeared as perplexed as I felt.

I looked back at June May in time to see Ruthie, with more hug obviously left in her, put her arms around Miz Newcomb's waist and hop a little jig into her skirts.

I turned my attention back to Teacher.

"Now June May will read her award-winning entry. June May is without question our most-improved student thus far in the school year. Her essay was chosen for her use of the topic—the children were asked to write about an important person in his or her life—and her use of language. It's a poem as lovely as—"

Teacher blushed fierce as fever. "Well, I suppose you might say it's as pretty as a nickel postcard. June May?"

Applause filled the room to the rafters. I listened to June May's words with wonder and pride.

GRANNY VIRGINIA GRANT DICKE

By June May Justice

We see her once a year—
July 4, cousins, root beer.
Her eyes spark-snap secrets.
We eat too much good talk play.
Come shadowy dark we
wagon-pile and hay-sleep smile.
Poppa sings us late-late to home.
Someday soon we'll meet again.

The end.

MORE APPLAUSE. JUNE MAY CURTSIED two, three times. Where on God's green did she learn that? Never mind where did she learn to read and write so pretty. As the shouts and whistles swarmed around her, June May held up one nearly clean little hand, much like Teacher might do.

"I just want to say 'thank you' to Miz Newcomb, the momma of Mary Grace Newcomb, for helping me so much." She paused like she was looking into the eyes of each person there. "Not everybody's good right off at everything." June May's voice was clear and strong, not whispy-dreamy like usual.

"For the longest time I couldn't make no, I mean, any, sense of the squiggles and marks on pages. It got so I didn't even want to try. But Miz Newcomb showed me how it's better to expect something good, like a visit from Mrs. President Rosebelt, than to fear something bad. And I want to make sure my friend Possum remembers that."

June May curtsied again and went back toward her seat, with parents and kids alike clapping her on the back and grinning like they were all winners.

Not a few people stared at me too.

I let go of Mary Grace's hand. For once, I was glad when she acted the cotton queen. She made her way over to her folks, looking pink as punch and twice as pleased, as if she'd taught June May herself. A few kids grinned at Mary Grace that I knew had never looked at her but cross-eyed all year.

Mister Newcomb smiled and shook hands with some parents I bet hadn't said ten words to him since he took over the store, but he kept his left hand on his wife's shoulder.

As the happy hive sounds of the room finally quieted, Teacher spoke once more. "I have one more essay I'd like for you to hear tonight. Although it is not the prizewinner, it is an essay that shows a great amount of personal improvement and growth on the part of two of my students. Although this is rather unusual, I will have a third person read the essay. Afterward, as we enjoy punch and cookies, I am sure 'more will be revealed,' if the players choose to share their tale." She cleared her throat.

I thought she winked. I don't suppose a person in the room had any idea what she was about to say. "Tully Spencer!"

I hadn't even seen him till he made his way forward. It looked like he'd had a bath, but I couldn't read anything else about him. I didn't think he'd written an essay, and I for sure didn't think he deserved to win a prize after what he did, so I was triple-double surprised when he turned to us.

What he read sounded familiar.

Real familiar. For a reason.

It was the essay me and Mary Grace had written and turned in with the "found" book.

I looked around for Mary Grace. We shared surprise between us, like a pair of woke-up winter badgers. I couldn't see my own face, but hers was beetier than beets.

I realized something else too. Mary Grace Newcomb had called me "Possum."

To Miss Teacher

Wrong isn't always all wrong.

**Somebody might do wrong
but mean right.**

Like Miz Newcomb says, Mrs. President Roosevelt
has the best manners, and she likely would give a
person a chance to explain if they did something
that seemed all wrong.

**Because you can't always believe
what you see or hear.**

If you're on one side of a strong punch
or strong words
you can't know how they land
on the other side.

Sometimes we don't see
even when things are up in our faces
**because we're too busy looking
at the wrong things.**

A person might be proud
or stubborn

and right
or wrong
and still say
I'm sorry
or I forgive you.
And mean it.

The
End.

IT TOOK A GREAT DEAL of explaining all around—and every sip of punch in the bowl—for the full stories of Tully, June May, Mary Grace, me, and Miz Newcomb to be told and retold.

Mary Grace and I admitted to writing the essay that Tully read. Mary Grace, as usual, trying to hog all the credit for the idea and the work. To hear her tell it, we acted like detectives to solve the mystery and like missionaries to save Tully's hide.

Wasn't how I might have told it, but I had to admit she had a certain way with a yarn.

Tully admitted he had taken the book to quit us girls quarreling. "I never wanted to lose you as my best friend, Possum," he said. He handed me a grimy, folded sheet of paper before taking Mary Grace's hand and slipping off to talk to Miz Newcomb.

I went looking for June May to find out more about those secret lessons of hers and to take a closer look at her prize. I guess it should not have surprised me that June May could find a way to get at Miz Newcomb.

I sidled up to get a closer look at Miz Newcomb as she spoke with Tully and Mary Grace. She didn't seem nearly as crazy as that first time I saw her. Seeing Miz Newcomb so happy and lively made me realize that most likely she suffers from the sadness at times. Sadness is a grief that can make a person sick or crazy, and don't I know it.

Who would've thought Miz Newcomb and I might have something in common?

What's good to be reminded is sickness can get better. Seeing Mary Grace with her momma, I hoped that was true for them.

Who else did I know who was sick to unrecognition with the craziness of grief? Thinking of my own sweet daddy, I prayed there was hope for him too.

Plus, I realized June May'd also found a way to touch Mary Grace, which had to be harder even than talking to a sick cow. Mary Grace had good reason now to be proud of her momma, rather than ashamed.

Too bad she could not do anything for Daddy. Or me. Not even June May could find a way to reach those places that, at least until now, I could not.

Mary Grace and Tully had wandered off so she could talk at Miss Arthington. Good grief—clearly not everything else was changed to perfect.

Just then I heard June May calling me over and saw her swinging on Miz Newcomb's arm. I felt shy and wordless. I tried to think and came up with, "Thanks for helping June May. I bet you're real proud of her."

I was church-truth glad June May had won and also knew she'd loan me the book so I could read to Momma on spring nights to come.

With a screech, June May left us to go barrel over a bunch of her brothers and left me and Miz Newcomb alone.

Miz Newcomb looked a little confused and panicked for a second, like a doe that hears a tick tock, but then smiled real big at me and waved a lacy little fan in front of her face. "As my friend Eleanor has said so often, there is something to the notion that, more often than not, one gets what one expects."

Then she winked at me, I swear, and leaned in to whisper: "But I best get home now. I'm gonna fix up some tea and—Well, who's to say the future First Lady might not be stopping by sometime soon."

WHEN THAT NIGHT WAS OVER and I lay in bed, my eyes were full with the shine of the evening. I rolled over and whispered, "Trav?"

He had looked asleep, but right away he lifted his head and thumped his tail.

"Good boy. Grab my coveralls, Trav."

He looked at me like he wondered where I thought I was fixing to go in the middle of a cold night, but that good dog did like he was told.

I fished into the pocket for the paper Tully had given me—his essay. In the moonlight from the window, I read it two, then three times.

As I fell asleep, I heard June May's words: "It's better to expect something good than to fear something bad."

What good, I wondered, could I expect?

Chapter 17

COME ALL YE

Christmas Eve seems made to be full of possibility.

I fetched carrots from the sand barrel under the porch and left them washed on the sideboard for Daddy. I'd hoped to catch a whiff of summer in their bright color but was disappointed. They smelled a bit earthy, like the last of autumn.

I had something to talk over with Momma, so I went out to the pecan tree.

Back to the kitchen, Daddy was chopping up those carrots to bake with honey; it was the dish Miz Justice agreed we could bring, on account of how much her boys like carrots. After supper, we'd all go on to church.

"Daddy," I said, "I've thought about it long and hard, and I think we should give Baby's clothes to Miz Justice for their new little fixing-to-be-a-baby-soon."

Daddy stopped chopping but kept his back to me.

"You hear me, Daddy? The clothes Momma made."

He still didn't turn. "What makes you think that's your decision to make, girl?" His voice was rough, and that was not what I had expected, not in the spirit of Christmas at all.

I had thought he'd be glad to be shed of the reminders of Momma and Baby, since he was so intent on acting like we never even had two people that we loved and lost and could go on missing for forever, which was about how it seemed.

Still, what I said was, "Don't be that way, Daddy. We don't need that tin of sweet things. It's not doing us any good except maybe to make us sad remembering better times, and you know well as me the Justices haven't got but two rags to tie together to put that baby into."

Daddy turned and leaned against the counter, hugging himself so each orange-tinted hand slipped under the opposite arm. He squinted like seeing me for the first time. "You know how many hours your momma put into them tiny things, sittin' out back under that tree?"

I swallowed hard and stood up straight. "Yes, sir," I said, "so many that she'd want them not to go to waste."

I had to keep going.

"Daddy, as much change as we've had around here, maybe you'd like to forget there ever was a Momma or Baby. If it would make the hurting stop, I maybe would too, but I can't. I can't turn around without feeling Momma because she's in me, in us. She's part of us. We don't need a biscuit tin to remind us who she was. We don't need it."

"Possum!" Daddy picked up the chopping knife and threw it into the dishwater with a dull plop. "How can you have any idea what I need when I don't know myself?"

I wanted to run to him, but my feet rooted. Trav came to stand by my side; surely he did not know this white-faced, whiter-lipped man staring me down. I certainly did not.

My hand brushed Trav's neck, and I felt his hair up.

"I don't know myself," Daddy repeated, voice so low I could barely tell his from the growl coming up deep in Trav. He turned, stiff as a lead soldier, and went out the door. I heard the door of his shop open and close.

When I remembered to shut my gaping mouth, I started getting ready to go out, trembling the whole time like birch in autumn. When it was time, I stood outside the shop and called, "I'm fixin' to go now." Church-truth, I wasn't sure if I wanted him to answer, but he didn't, so we'll never know.

I wished I could split myself in two or disappear altogether, but neither of those seemed likely miracles with God so busy for Christmas and all. So instead I told Trav to stay put and keep an eye on things, and I took myself out of there.

CHRISTMAS AT THE JUSTICES' was something to see, not the least being all those boys lined up like a fence getting taller by the picket—or shorter, depending on how you looked at them.

Only Jump at the far end seemed to stand out to me for some reason, maybe because his outgrown bib overalls, though clean and pressed as usual, seemed too short for his arms and legs. His worn, patched shirt was too small too, and he looked lean and strong as a racehorse underneath it. I don't know why I hadn't noticed it before, but his curly eyelashes were as thick as horsetails around marble-green eyes.

It was a revelation, and I might have lingered on it if June May hadn't been jumping all over to show me the Christmasing of their home.

The house was strung up with every kind of greenery at the windows and on the tables so it smelled like piney forest. In the corner stood a fine proud tree, which the littlest boys told me they had cut and drug home themselves. It near brushed the ceiling even before they put on a tin star. The tree was done up with popcorn balls and red crab-apple ropes and paper chains that June May and I had colored red or green or left white and glued into links with flour paste.

Momma and I had done up our tree each year

pretty as a twelve-point buck, but this year Daddy hadn't even brought one home. I could've felled one for us, but what was the point? I didn't think I'd miss it either, till I was standing in that warm, glowing room full of Justices and all the sounds and smells of a happy family that was more bound together than torn apart.

With a pang, I wished Daddy was there with me and not home being someone I barely knew. Then I heard in my head that awful voice and felt a chill. I was nothing but relieved when Miz Justice called over the noise, "Well, what you all waitin' for? Food's not gonna eat itself."

THAT MEAL WAS ONE FOR history books, I swear. I thought I was pretty good, planting and weeding the garden and cooking and cleaning and even helping keep the wood box filled. Still, I could see it was handy to have a boy or six around to catch grouse and snowshoe hares or jackrabbits. I can shoot squirrels and catch fish just fine. Church-truth, I do not care for the gutting, though I don't mind burying entrails in the garden. And I do enjoy a fine fresh fish dredged in flour and fried in lard—so crispy brown outside. Mm.

June May had put the jawbreaker I gave her into a pocket, and during dinner, she kept taking it out and looking at it. "Possum, what kind of candy you figure a cow would eat?"

You had to stay alert to keep up with June May. "You mean like would Dusty eat root-beer barrels?" How could she even think of such things with all that people-food making the table groan?

She turned to look at me. "Root-beer barrels would cut her tongue!"

I shook my pigtails to behind my back. Miz Justice had done them up real nice, like Momma used to. "What you gettin' at, June May?"

She smiled. "I was pondering," she said, "would Dusty ruther have hay candy or grass candy?"

I was saved from answering this riddle when Miz Justice said, "Let's leave the table to clear and sit by the tree a bit."

"I'll get the chicory coffee, Ma," said Jessup.

"No, I'll get it," said Jarvis, and shoved his twin.

"Boys!" said Miz Justice, strong but somehow without yelling. They froze. "It's Christmas. What would your pa say?"

They hung their heads. Jump said, "Pa'd say, 'Jarvis get the coffee, Jessup get the milk, and the next one who fights on Christmas gets coal in his stocking.'"

Everyone laughed then, even me. I hadn't realized Jump was getting so wise. Also, had his voice always been like July honey straight from the comb?

I guess I could have listened to it all day. If I had a mind to.

We moved to sit around the tree, and June May, like to explode with excitement, dragged me to it. What I had not noticed was that under the tree was a pretty package of butcher paper that looked to have been colored by some of the smaller Justices, and it had my name on it. It was the only. parcel under the tree.

I stared and stared until Miz Justice had to say, real gentle, "Go on, Possum."

Folded neatly was a cotton jumper in red paisley on yellow, just my size and pretty as an orchard of ripe apples. Underneath it was a jumpsuit of flying geese against a fall blue sky. I knew them at once as coming from Momma's dresses that Daddy had given to Miss Arthington.

As I held up one piece in each hand, I heard a couple of the boys wolf-whistle, like from way far off.

"But—"

I stared at the dresses like they might sprout teeth and snap off my arm.

"It wasn't easy, Possum." Miz Justice's voice reached my slow-hearing, ringing ears. "She tried her best. Like we all do." The stitches did not have the precision I knew to be Miz Justice's work, though the dresses seemed sturdy enough. Then it came to me. Miss Arthington! Daddy gave her Momma's dresses to fix up for me?

At that moment, I was flooded so full of comprehension there was no room left for words. I wished more than ever that Daddy was there and that we'd had a package for Baby Justice under that tree.

I wanted to cry, wishing to take back every mean thing I'd ever felt and thought. I might have too, if June May hadn't been dancing all around me in excitement—"Try it on, Possum! Possum's got a dress!"—and taken that moment to nearly knock over the tree, tin star and all.

Yet that was not to be the biggest surprise of the night.

In all the commotion of the tree nearly a-tipping, no one except the dogs heard the front door open and close.

When we all turned to see about the baying and barking, the laughter turned to screams and tears as a blur of Justices ran to the door and nearly trampled the dogs that had nearly trampled Mister Justice, who looked stunned like he'd just won a pie-eating contest, only not as sick. All the children climbed him like he was the sturdiest oak, arms waving every which way. He rubbed heads and hugged boys and kissed June May.

Then Mister Justice looked up and let his eyes wander to the table and fix on Miz Justice with her hands on her belly. The children quieted and parted, and with four quick strides, he covered the distance to her. He grabbed Miz Justice into such a lock that, had it gone on a second longer, I might have feared for their air supply.

I don't think Mister Justice saw me, rooted as I was, for his family filling his eyes with love.

THE MORNING COME

The Justices shared our lives in so many ways, it was hard to think of them not being family. Yet on that night, seeing them all happy together made me feel strange in my gut, and I was secret-glad when it was time to leave for church.

The walk was itself as beautiful as a church. It was cold enough to see your breath and hear shoes crunch frost, yet we didn't feel a lick of cold, stuffed as we were with Christmas dinner and excitement and holiness.

The sky was so dark that all God's lanterns seemed as bright as the one those kings must've followed to Bethlehem.

Outside, a little ways from the church door, stood one person with two heads. As we got closer I saw it was a moon-eyed couple whispering and giggling in the starlight. A few steps more, and I heard a clear-bell musical laugh that I knew. It was Miss Arthington, pink-cheeked and eyes flashing like I had never seen her. But the fellow she was with, looking fine in a dandy hat and wool coat, I had never seen the likes of before.

"LizBetty Porter," said Miss Arthington, sounding prim and done up, even for her. "This is Nevin Charlesworth. Mister Charlesworth, may I present LizBetty Porter, one of my students."

He held out his hand to shake. I was relieved to see he wasn't so citified as to wear gloves. Good, firm grip—though the skin felt softer than any fella's I knew. Nice smile. Good teeth.

"It's a pleasure, Miss Porter." He gave me a little bow as he released my hand.

"Are you Teacher's fancy from New York?" Toad! It popped out before I had a chance to stop it. My fists curled a bit to think he was the one who had made her cry so with his fancy letters. What could he have said so cruel?

"LizBetty!" Teacher looked pink and piqued, but the man grinned.

"Miss Arthington has told me so much about all of her students, I feel as if I know you myself." His voice reminded me of something smooth and good to eat. "She's quite fond of you all, and now that I am meeting some of her charges, I can see why. I realize how hard it will be for her to say good-bye come spring."

"Nevin Charlesworth!" Teacher's face got pinker. "Why don't you wait for me inside?"

He tipped his head at me, brushed the brim of

his hat, and disappeared into the lamplight glow spilling from the church.

"Say good-bye? What did he mean, Miss Arthington? You going on a trip?"

Before I could spot her changing the subject, Teacher quickly explained that this fellow's unexpected visit was why she had not been at the Justices' that night to see me open my present.

"Missus Justice was simply too busy to do the work herself, so I hope you don't mind that I—Well, I tried my best." She ducked her head and then looked at me from under her fat eyelashes. She asked shyly: "Was it all right?"

"All right?" I asked, remembering the look on everybody's, on Jump's, face when I tried one of the dresses on. I grabbed her around the middle in a barrel hug and muffled into her coat. I whispered, "They're the most beautiful dresses I've ever seen."

Miss Arthington and I then were nearly bowled over by the blur that was June May, hopping around trying to introduce her pa.

I went into the church alone and feeling numb despite the bells that rang us into the golden warm. People who barely raised an eyebrow the rest of the year welcomed each other in voices joyful but hushed as they passed the live Nativity put on as usual by the preacher's kids.

I saw pants sticking out below Joseph's robe. One of the Wise Men had the raw-nose end of a bad cold, and Mary's tinfoil halo tilted like to fall, but then I caught sight of the manger of straw, with the Baby Jesus on top wrapped in swaddling feed sacks and laughing as he tried to kick free his holy little feet.

Suddenly, I saw Momma under that halo and Daddy holding that staff and my own sweet brother Baby in that manger, and something broke loose inside of me, like Babel crashing from my heart into my stomach, and roaring in my ears. The salt-fire of tears licked at my eyelids, and I pushed past the choir and out the side door for giant gulps of air.

I don't know how long I stayed on my knees, but they were like to freeze, and it seemed I'd been pounding solid earth with my fists when I thought I felt the hand of God grab my shoulder and pull me into a rocking, back-breaking hold.

I tried to stop crying but heard my own ragged sobs like cloth tearing. All our arms shook with grief and sorrow. Then somehow I knew it wasn't God holding me but my own sweet daddy, and us both crying for Momma and Baby and GrandNam and ourselves, and I tried to hold him as tight as he was holding me.

At first, that sadness seemed unstoppable, like the creek rising in rain, and it plain needed exorcising.

From the church I heard the piano lady starting "Silent Night," which it certainly was not where we were, but slowly voices joined in like a train of music getting closer, then fading. Next was "O Come, All Ye Faithful," and more voices slipped through the cracks of the old church and floated like prayers up into the black night.

Gradually, our sounds got quieter as our hearts grew fuller with love and acceptance. When the music stopped, one of my ears heard murmuring from the church. Daddy at last sat hard on the ground and scooped me into his lap. He wiped his face with his sleeve and gave me a soggy, sad smile and wiped my face with his other sleeve, and he smelled like soap and smoke, and then we sat, his head on mine.

The piano started up again, and after a minute, you knew it was the children singing "Away in a Manger" so sweet and pure as to fix a world of hurts.

I looked around us in the half-dark and saw at our feet the biscuit tin that held Baby's clothes.

And right then, clear as the night was night, I knew everything would be all right.

I FELT LIKE I HAD been awake all night with the wonder of all that had happened. I don't guess I slept more than two or three winks before I opened one eye and saw the pink-gray of dawn putting on its face powder. It had a magical feel to it, that time of morning and the crisp air and the silence.

I sat up in my bed and whispered, "Traveler, 'ya bo'." He crawled out from under the bed like he'd been waiting for me, and I *ch-ch'kd* him onto the bed, where he was usually not allowed. He tilted his head.

"Come on," I said. "It's Christmas."

He jumped up and sat next to me. I wrapped GrandNam's quilt 'round us both. I felt Traveler's fur on my arm and the warmth of his breath mixed with what I was sure was the smell of GrandNam making Sunday breakfast. Maybe it was a dream, but a good one.

I rubbed a circle out of the steam and frost on the window, and together we watched that Christmas morning commence with colors to rival any Baptist window. I knew it was a special gift, just for me.

"Thank you, Momma," I whispered, like a prayer. "I know you've done this, all this, bringing Daddy back to Daddy. Helping me make a friend of that crazy Mary Grace Newcomb. Leading me to a teacher who knows, like you do, that learning is more than schooling. I fought so hard to do what I thought you wanted, but going to school is opening the world for me. And wait till you see the books Miz Newcomb has. We're never gonna stop learning, Momma, not ever. And maybe I'll even go to college someday so I can show other kids how much better learning is than schooling. I'm sorry if I embarrassed you by not winning the essay contest, but I'm real proud of June May, and maybe you had something to do with that too. I love you, Momma. Merry Christmas, Baby."

Just then, my stomach let out a growl that made Traveler yip, and he jumped out from our tent of covers and trotted toward the kitchen. I grabbed my clothes and followed, knowing it'd be warmer to dress near the old Monarch stove.

Trav beat me and was already curled at the foot of the stove, soaking in the warmth. Though his eyes were closed, I knew he was more than ready to clean up any spills that might accidentally find their way into his path.

I found Daddy making his special breakfast of popovers with eggs and a bit of whipped cream. It's something he did often before Momma died but had not at all since. Bacon sizzled and popped in the skillet. I felt a churning in my stomach of hunger and happiness mixed with anticipation.

Something about Christmas just does that to a person.

I was clearing the table when Jump came over to visit, first off hemming and hawing, then stuttering, and then saying what I did not expect:

"I'n't that something about Miss Arthington fixin' to get hitched and go back to New York and all, after all them letters she got and all that cryin' she did? Yankees sure are funny strange."

His voice had gone, but I had no idea why he was carrying on. And on Christmas too. Not to mention the whole time with his arms wound around like he got put together backward.

"Jumper Justice," I said, feeling a very un–Christmasy kind of cross. "Did you come all the way over here to talk gossip after not having ten words to say for, oh, I don't know how long?"

He got red-faced then and said, "Here," as he shoved the newspaper-wrapped bundle at me. Wouldn't even look me in the eye. *When did he get so shy?* I wondered, feeling a mite shy myself.

Turned out to be a brand-new flip, made himself. He cut the handle out of a board instead of a regular tree fork and painted it a pretty green and white. Even had my name carved onto it—"LIZBETTY."

"You feelin' all right, Possum?" My face warmed to think he'd seen me acting the loony bird the night before. To think he'd noticed me at all.

Daddy came upon us, clearing his throat real loud. "Why don't you get on home to your folks, now, boy? Christmas is time for family."

I held up my flip. "Look, Daddy, look at my name. Isn't it beautiful?"

Daddy cleared his throat again.

I hoped he wasn't getting sick.

"I reckon we'll have to see if it shoots as pretty as it looks."

"Oh, it does sure, sir." His voice was a tad on

the loud side. "Myself I took down three of my brothers' pop bottles before I brung it over, jes' to be sure. It's true, awright."

Jump talked to Daddy, but he was looking straight into me. He added, "'Course, anyone's as good a shot as Possum ain't gonna have trouble with any kinda flip." He grinned at me and winked.

"I'm sure Possum'll give it a go later. Now off with you, Jumper Justice, afore I try it on you myself. I got my own present to give to my daughter."

Daddy put extra butter and syrup on the words "my daughter."

Another present! Jump disappeared faster than sin on Sunday. I was so excited I almost didn't notice.

Daddy took my hand and led me outside, and there was the prettiest bench, just my size. Room for Trav underneath. "It's for you to sit outside, under the trees," he said, his voice rough. If he was getting sick, I'd need to see Miss Eulah for a cure.

So much carving and delicate work. On the back was a golden sun rising over our mountains; I could pick out each peak. On the opposite side was a cunning carving of our holler, house and shed and path and stream. And Momma's tree. But in the center, between the house and the mountains, stood four figures facing the sun. The man had an arm around the woman's waist. The woman had a baby slung on her hip. And between the two adults stood a fourth figure, a tall girl in glumpy pigtails. Wearing a dress—but no shoes.

"Oh, Daddy." I could say no more.

Here was hours and hours of Daddy's love made solid for me. Here was my family. This was what he had been working on so long in his shop, keeping me away. Just this. Just this gift of his heart.

I grabbed him around the neck to kiss his cheek—wasn't as far a stretch as it used to be. Then I sat on my bench to try it on for size. Perfect. I jumped up and hugged him again. "Oh, Daddy, I'm so sorry for—"

"Hush now." He lifted me and spun me around, and when he did, my heart felt as light as my feet.

When he let me go, his watery eyes looked into mine, themselves full of happy tears. He put a hand on either side of my face and stared. "I see Noralee in you, honey bunch, the best of her and, I hope, of me."

I hoped I'd be that lucky. I suspected I was.

Then he stepped back and wiped his face on his shirt, shook his head, and nodded toward the pecan tree. "Want help with that?"

I looked at my beautiful bench and then at the tree. "No, thank you, Daddy. I can manage." I knew I could.

Then I picked up my bench and marched right down to Momma's tree. I explained to her I'd be putting this bench in my own spot. It seemed right to keep open the space beneath the pecan.

Under the peach tree, on the east side of the house, would be a fine place to sit and watch the morning come.

I heard GrandNam say plenty of times that the road to perdition was paved with good intentions.

I don't guess I ever thought on what the road to Heaven might be paved with.

But as I sat on my bench, I finally knew one answer.

A COUPLE OF DAYS AFTER CHRISTMAS, Daddy said he thought, in the spirit of the season, he might call on Miz Pickerel. He looked worried when he said it, like he expected one of those ugly toads to hop out of my mouth, but all I felt was my heart squeezed with love, and I knew he deserved to feel that again too. Wasn't my place to keep him from it anyway.

"I think that's a fine idea, Daddy." And he smiled like the sun coming out. Momma wanted us to keep smiling. I made sure he wore his good coveralls.

Around toward dusk, Jump came by and asked did I want to go frog gigging with him.

Did I? "Last one there's a rotten egg." I took off running. When we got near the creek, I ran ahead and slid down the muddy bank, laughing.

Jump was right behind.

"Possum." His voice took on a serious tone I didn't know if I could get used to, his face a question mark. "Can I ask you somethin'?"

My throat and stomach traded places.

"'Course, Jump."

"You ever wonder—them tadpokes. Where do you s'pose those tails go?"

➤ AFTERWORD ❧

Maria D. Laso (whose nickname was Mari Lou) was my wife for the last twenty-six years of her life. This lovely book is her legacy.

Mari Lou loved to read at an early age. She read the classics throughout high school, and her strong vocabulary helped prepare her for a copy-editing career in newspapers. But she always loved reading children's books and someday hoped to write one.

She eventually started creating clever picture books and short stories. She mixed wordplay with life lessons, but her priority was a middle grade novel with the working title *The Morning Come*. She spent months sketching out the story, which centered on a young girl nicknamed Possum in the Deep South in 1932 during the Great Depression. Mari Lou researched that time and place extensively and began to flesh out her characters: Daddy, Miss Arthington, Tully, June May, but most of all LizBetty, "otherwise known as Possum." In Possum,

Mari Lou found a kindred spirit, a feisty girl who spoke her mind, had a wicked sense of humor, was fiercely loyal to her friends and family, and didn't suffer fools gladly—which come to think of it, sounds just like my wife.

As I would read the drafts of her story month by month, year by year, I marveled that this had all sprung from Mari Lou's far-reaching imagination. The setting and adventures were nothing like her own childhood, so she was truly letting her mind run free. She felt compelled to take Possum through these encounters en route to learning about life and love.

Mari Lou worked on this story for almost a decade. At about the same time she was close to finishing the book, she grew seriously ill. As her strength and focus weakened, she managed to complete her final edits with the loving, devoted help of friend and fellow writer Dawne Knobbe, who got to know the story and characters almost as well as Mari Lou did.

Mari Lou passed away in September 2015, but she took comfort in knowing that her wonderful story would be published and read by young people of all ages. I am so proud of what she accomplished.

It is sad that Mari Lou won't be able to create further amazing adventures, but I know that she would hope that Possum's endearing and enduring spirit will inspire others to create adventures of their own.

—Stephen Elders

⇒ ABOUT *the* AUTHOR ⇐

A former journalist, Maria D. Laso was a beloved
creative writing teacher in Orange County, California,
where she helped people from teens to senior citi-
zens find their voices. She completed her debut
novel, *Otherwise Known as Possum*, shortly before
her death in 2015.